9

Welcome to WAHOO

Welcome to WAHOO

Dennis and Elise Carr

BLOOMSBURY

T 7093

Published by Bloomsbury Publishing, New York, London, and Berlin
Distributed to the trade by Holtzbrinck Publishers

Library of Congress Cataloging-in-Publication Data
Carr, Dennis.
Welcome to Wahoo / by Dennis and Elise Pritcher Carr.
p.   cm.
Summary: Having been told that she must leave her European
boarding school to live in Nebraska under an assumed name to protect her
from Mafia assassins, Victoria Van Wyck makes a real friend and tries
to stop a smear campaign directed at her by the school's popular clique.
ISBN-10: 1-58234-696-8 • ISBN-13: 978-1-58234-696-0
[1. Conduct of life—Fiction.   2. Friendship—Fiction.   3. Gossip—Fiction.
4. High schools—Fiction.   5. Schools—Fiction.]   I. Carr, Elise Pritcher.
II. Title.
PZ7.C22932Wel 2006   [Fic]—dc22   2005030954

First U.S. Edition 2006
Printed in the U.S.A.
2   4   6   8   10   9   7   5   3   1

Bloomsbury Publishing, Children's Books, U.S.A.
175 Fifth Avenue, New York, NY 10010

All papers used by Bloomsbury Publishing are natural, recyclable products
made from wood grown in well-managed forests. The manufacturing
processes conform to the environmental regulations of the country of origin.

Welcome to WAHOO

CHAPTER 1

Me

My name is Victoria Julianne Van Wyck. My friends call me Jewels because of my family's money; the European press calls me "Brat" or "La Terreur Américain"—and that's on good days. My mother calls me Victoria: "You were named after a queen, the least you can do is act like a lady" (yeah, right), and my father mostly just calls me "you," as in: "What sort of trouble have *you* got yourself into this time?"

This is a rather narrow-minded overreaction to what I would describe as my natural thirst for adventure.

Just because Daddy's spent several hundred thousand Swiss Francs (which is only one or two hundred thousand American dollars) bailing me out of trouble in Germany, France, and Italy for indiscretions a more forgiving father would write off to youthful exuberance doesn't mean I'm a bad person. Even a judge in Monaco termed me "high-spirited" after a group of us broke into the local zoo and released a dozen monkeys into the Four Seasons grand ballroom. It was hilarious (though I might have conked a gendarme with a bottle of champagne—I can't remember).

But enough of that.

This story begins months ago, right after my seventeenth birthday.

School was ever so tedious, and I needed to blow off steam.

Unfortunately, I was stuck in L'École Suisse/Américain, a posh boarding school for girls from wealthy families. You may have heard of it; the two tabloid hotel heiresses once attended, but I'm not giving them any more publicity since: a) I don't like them, and b) they're dumber than *pâte de foie gras*, which comes out of a goose and is way overrated. L'École Suisse sits high above Lake Lucerne, in what travel agents refer to as the coolest ski spot in Switzerland. United States senators, European rulers, and Hollywood big shots send their daughters to be educated—more like babysat—as class attendance is not mandatory and grades can be finessed (a French word meaning "corrupted").

I know all about corruption now, having practically

grown up here. Eight years is a long time to be in any institution, even one as gilded as this.

The trouble started ten days into my junior year. I had just received a reprimand from the floor monitor for my second curfew violation, which meant automatic detention. (Ugh!) On top of which, I got a hideous letter from Mother.

Dear Victoria,

The flower garden looks promising this year, and Viv Rothchild says I should let Home and Hearth magazine onto the estate to photograph the dahlias. What do you think, dear?

Oh, I had Botox on my forehead from a marvelously creepy Swedish doctor recommended by Nan Sunderland. I look ten years younger—that's what Nan says. Almost forgot—we went to a party thrown by the Duke of Bellingham—talk about a man in need of facial paralysis. By the way, how are you getting on? Must dash. Be sure to write.

Love, Mother

P.S. Your father is suspending your banking privileges for three weeks. Sorry, pet. Though after your latest indiscretion in Cannes, I can't say I blame him. What are we to do with you, dearest?

I will try to manage a visit soon—how long has it been, four months? Time flies. XXOO

I decided, with the encouragement of my English roommate, Stella, to burn the letter, exorcising the bad karma contained therein.

Pop. Into the trash can it went, and as the lovely flames subsided, Stella and I skipped out toward the common room in search of mischief, adventure, or chocolate—whichever came first. We had only been there a few minutes when the senior proctor rushed in.

"Fire!" she yelled.

"Uh-oh," I said.

The rest of the dorm began to evacuate; I raced back upstairs. By the time I arrived on the fifth floor, thick, choking smoke had filled the hallway. The head-mistress and several staffers swarmed about my room, fire extinguishers whooshing.

It seems the window curtains had caught fire . . . imagine that.

"You are restricted to your room for the next month, Miss Van Wyck," Mistress barked. "You know the rules about smoking in the dorm."

I was about to deny that I smoked (which I don't), when Genevieve, the Swiss girl from the room next door, stumbled inside, blubbering. In her arms, she held her hateful little yap dog terrier, named—inappropriately—Serenity.

"She's fallen off the balcony—look—her leg's broken."

Serenity howled on cue as Genevieve turned to me. "The fire must have panicked her. This is all your fault." Sob.

"How is it my fault you have a stupid dog?" It seemed a logical question.

Mistress shot me a malevolent look. "Make that *two* months restriction, Victoria. You never change, do you?"

Then she and her entourage whirled and stalked off, coughing.

I almost laughed. Then it hit me.

Two months?

No way!

I waited until they were out of sight, then dialed the cute French boy I'd met over the weekend. He told me his name was Jean Claude and that he descended from royalty (every French boy says that).

"Come get me," I said.

"Jump, darling."

Picture me sneaking down the fire escape, halfway between my fifth-story dorm room and the ground.

It's pitch-black midnight, and Jean Claude wants me to jump. (He's what Parisians would call an *imbécile*.)

He's sitting in my Mercedes with Stella, who's already made it down, but I'm the one being chased by the dorm security Nazi—Hildegard—and Frenchie wants me to vault into the air, land on soggy Swiss turf, and possibly break an ankle, or worse, the heel on my new pair of Giuseppe Zanotti pumps.

Merde!

So I hurry down the last fifteen feet and, at the bottom, use a trick every boarding school getaway artist knows—squirt lighter fluid up the metal ladder, then set it afire.

Voilà.

(Incidentally, I'm not a pyro. Don't get the wrong idea. These are just two isolated fire incidents . . . plus that one time in a Berlin nightclub—which was not my fault.)

So, Hildegard (shrewdly) spots the flames rushing toward her and scampers back onto the third floor landing.

I hop into the seat next to my pallid paramour and away we speed, heading for a night of big fun at Casino Lucerne.

A word here about European boys. The rich ones, no matter what nationality, have one thing in common—all they want is to do you. They might not know you, they might not even like you; the point is, you are a contest for them, nothing more. American girls are especially prized. Why? Because they hate the U.S. in Europe now, and what better way to show off their machismo than with your sexual humiliation.

My advice? Never, ever become a trophy. The moment you give in, the party's over. You're no longer Cinderella, you're the pumpkin.

My parents didn't teach me that, although they'd be happy to know I'm still a virgin.

Here's a guide to continental come-ons:

"*Ma petite chu-chu. Je t'adore.* I must kiss you, or I will die." That's the French way.

German boys are more direct. "You like me, ja?"

"I'm not throwing up yet, if that's what you mean."

"Then we do it. I haf fantastic body." (Notice how it's all about them.)

Swiss boys talk about money and the practical side of sex. "You should give yourself to someone of influence, like me. Then, you could have a brilliant future. What time is it?"

Some of my favorite lines come from the English upper class. "Shagging is ripper, luv. Keeps the motor running," or "If you refuse me now, I could become a pooftah, and it would be your bloody fault." Wrong!

Where was I? Oh, yes . . .

Jean Claude, Stella, and I arrived at the casino in a rush and were shown into the private baccarat room. As long as your family has money in Switzerland, no one cares if you are a couple of underage schoolgirls truant from the dorm.

We gambled, on credit, and sipped free champagne. I was winning, since I am—I say this without bragging—a superb gambler. It's an instinct.

Jean Claude attempted to distract me by fondling my derrière, but I kept him at bay with a few kicks to his skinny shins.

"I cannot keep my hands from you," he whispered as he put his tongue in my ear.

"Just keep your paws off my chips!" I spritzed champagne on the side of his face.

SPLASH.

(See how *he* likes a wet eardrum.)

He dried his head on the jacket of an accommodating waiter and returned to the table.

After an hour, I was up thirty thousand Swiss Francs, Jean Claude down about the same, and Stella long gone in the company of Count Somebody from Palermo. That's when the worst thing in the world happened—Adam appeared.

"Come along, Victoria. Your father wants a word."

"Can't you see I'm winning here?"

"Leave her alone," Jean Claude bluffed.

But Adam and the pit boss were already sweeping my chips into a casino deposit bag.

"Stop! 'Alf those chips are mine." Jean Claude lunged for the money—pig!

POW.

Adam's fist found its mark, and down the French boy fell. I laughed. Sometimes Adam can be a giggle.

"Are you coming the easy or the hard way, Vickie?"

I hate that nickname—rhymes with "icky," which I'm certainly not—but something about his steely expression convinced me he wasn't in the mood to be corrected, so I stepped over Jean Claude, and followed Adam out of the casino.

Someone always wants to stop me having fun.

CHAPTER 2

Me and Adam York

At twenty-five years old, Rhodes Scholar Adam York must have thought he had a bright future when my father hired him to work for Van Wyck International. Don't ask me what my father does—something to do with trading currency in a process called arbitrage (fleecing the unwary).

Adam is tall, lean, and kinda cute for an older man—he's thirty now—but is far too serious and has no sense of fun or imagination, since I'm sure when he was assigned to the Loss Prevention division he never imagined he'd end up having to chase me all over the continent, "rescuing" me from "Euro-trash playboys"—a term I don't care for, since I've met plenty of trashy playboys in New York and L.A.

When he pulled me from the casino, I could tell he was in one of his moods. All the way to the airport he remained silent, glancing at me only once to shoot a dagger stare when I said, in my most innocent voice, "I feel a headache coming on. Do you have any medication?"

We pulled onto the tarmac where my father's Gulfstream was fueled and ready for take-off. (Not a good sign. It suggested urgency, and one never wants urgent parents, since that invariably means trouble.) Adam shoved me up the gangway and ordered me to sit in the back—with all the engine noise.

He scowled. "I've got a ton of work to do. Try not to be a pest."

If he were the waiter at a five-star restaurant, I'd have had him fired. I took a nap instead.

Forty-eight minutes later, we touched down at fogbound Brussels airport, and a limousine carried us to the International Hôtel on Place Vendôme.

"Why are we stopping here?" I asked.

"Get out."

"But I don't have my clothes, toiletries—"

"All taken care of," he replied, pointing to a packed overnight bag. (Like I said, sometimes Adam is a hoot, the rest of the time he's a pain.)

The grand lobby was deserted at four in the morning, and so was the glass elevator whisking the driver, Adam, and me twenty flights skyward.

At the door to 2040, Adam turned to the chauffer. "Stand guard here. If she tries to leave, sit on her."

To me he said, "Your parents will be here in the morning. Stay put."

The room (not even a suite, mind you) was so nondescript I almost wanted to take up knitting. (Never.) No balcony, no chandelier, no Jacuzzi, no servants—it was a dump. I knew what I needed, but the minibar was empty.

I called room service—my room had been quarantined. I explained I needed wine on doctor's orders—hacking cough, emergency, blah, blah. I even feigned diplomatic hysteria.

"The king of Morocco arrives in TWENTY MINUTES! If you don't want an INTERNATIONAL INCIDENT, which will certainly result in your hotel being EXPELLED FROM TRAVELOCITY.COM, I suggest . . . Hello? Hello?"

The moron hung up on me, Adam must have gotten to him.

Damn.

This was becoming tiresome. I turned on the telly, but Belgian TV is dead boring, so I fell asleep on the

lumpy couch and dreamt about that Italian race car driver—what's his name—Berlusconi? I was in the cockpit with him racing the streets of the Italian Grand Prix. I kept saying, "Faster, faster . . ." Then we crashed, and I was thirsty.

"Victoria, wake up, sweetheart."

"Thirsty," I said as my eyes snapped open.

It was Mother, rubbing my cheek. A worry frown clung to her face.

"Do you want some water?" My father stood behind calling me "you" again.

"What?"

"You said you were thirsty. Do you need water?"

My head throbbed. It was the devil, no doubt, reminding me of that casino champagne.

"Yes, Father. And some aspirin, too, please." I sat up as he retreated to the minibar for Perrier.

"Get dressed, dear. We brought you traveling clothes."

Was that fear I detected in my mother's voice?

"It's so early," I managed.

"It's six-fifteen precisely," Father said, shoving the bottled water into my face.

I drank. It tasted good. "Think I'll have a bath."

He sat heavily, his tone practically operatic. "There

is simply no time. Your mother and I have distressing news. We'll talk as you dress."

"Look, Daddy (always say "Daddy" in your best little-girl voice when you sense trouble coming—trust me, it works).

"Be quiet and listen!"

(Oops.)

"Let me tell it, dearest, will you?" Mom pleaded.

"All right, but quickly, we need to dye her hair."

A shiver shot straight up my spine . . . dye my hair?

Father turned away. I pulled on the clothes they'd brought—a cashmere turtleneck, a gray pleated Cavalli skirt, and a black Chanel blazer. (I adore Chanel. I make her fitted jackets look sooo good.)

Mom blurted the story, with Father interrupting to add a detail here and there, or to cut her off altogether. It seems something had gone terribly wrong with Daddy's business. When Mother uttered the word "disaster," my mind shut down. I watched through a haze as she fluttered about the room, jabbering and flapping her arms, while Father stood to one side, arms folded, glaring at me as if it were all my fault.

". . . embezzled company funds . . . persons unknown . . . bank foreclosure . . . hundreds of millions lost . . . the Sicilians blame your father."

That brought me up short. "Gangster money?" I tried.

"Hush," Father replied.

Long story short—the Cosa Nostra had decided to kill the Van Wyck family as revenge—which meant me too!

"W-Why don't we just go to the police?" I stammered.

"Because we'd be dead in an hour," Father said.

The little shiver in my spine was now a full-blown shake, rattle, and roll.

Adam walked in wearing a face like an undertaker. He carried two suitcases, which he set next to me.

"So w-what do we . . . do?" My voice had changed to an adolescent squeak.

"Disappear," Father said.

Mother began crying—no, sobbing.

I never imagined I'd see such a thing. Father pulled a wad of American money from his pocket, handing it to Adam. "This is our last five thousand dollars. Every account is frozen; it will have to do."

Then, he did the unspeakable. He dug into my purse, found my wallet, yanked out every single credit card (including my black American Express), and cut them up.

That's when I lashed out. "Do you mean to say that

after years of telling me to be a good girl, *you* were doing business with criminals? Hypocrite!"

"Victoria—," Mother blubbered.

Father interrupted. "Is that what you think of me?"

The expression on his face was not anger, far from it. He actually appeared wounded, and this cut more deeply than any rebuke could have.

When Father does get angry, there are never shouts or temper outbursts. He simply becomes glacial, and the room temperature drops to zero.

I bit my tongue, avoiding his stare.

A million troubling questions buzzed inside my head. Then my stomach decided to join the party, forcing me to run to the sink and vomit.

Mother blew her nose. "You'll have to go back to America, sweetheart; lay low for a year or two. Adam will look after you."

Adam's expression was as sour as my throat. What must he be thinking? I rinsed, then wiped my mouth. This was all happening way too fast.

"What if we—"

"Don't attempt to contact anyone you know, do you understand?" Father said.

I nodded, wondering if any of my friends would miss me. God, this was hideous, like being pushed down a well. My hands trembled, my knees felt rubbery.

I saw tears glisten on my mother's cheeks. As she dabbed them away, Father put his arm around her and closed his eyes. I felt his pain like a stiletto in my heart. A curtain descended over my vision. Only Adam's bright, steady gaze kept me from fainting.

"We'll be in touch as soon as possible." Father kissed me on the forehead, and it left an icy burn even as Mother's warm hand squeezed mine.

I think I began to pray. (Was I a hypocrite? Yes.)

Mother put her wet cheek next to mine. "Do what Adam says. We're going far away, darling; take care of yourself."

And just like that, they were out the door.

It was too much. I threw up again on the pillowcase, Perrier bubbles burning my nose on the way back out.

Then I heard a commotion in the hallway—shouts, banging. It sounded like one of those stupid Hollywood movies—or was it Mother and Father arguing? Without thinking, I ran to the door and flung it open. What I saw made me wish I were blind. At the end of the long corridor stood two men carrying machine guns—Uzis, I think they're called. They were kicking down every door looking for . . . me! How did I know this? Because just like in your nightmares when you're running away from the monster and you stop for a last peek, sure enough, the monster sees you, and now you're running again. That's what happened. One of the gunmen spotted me, muttered something to his mate, and they both started toward me like hellhounds. Adam dragged me back into the room, slamming and locking the door behind.

"Quick, down the fire escape!" he yelled.

Now, I don't scare easily, but I was so frightened I actually peed my pants—just a little drop, but there it was. I was too terrified to be embarrassed. A blast of cold air hit my face as Adam pushed me out the window. "Move!" he yelled.

Twenty floors up on a slick metal fire escape was not where I wanted to be. The first step nearly did me in when my foot slid wide. I looked down to the rain-swept street two hundred feet below.

"I can't . . . I . . ."

Adam kept nudging me with the suitcases. "Don't slow down!" He was probably enjoying this.

Something in me steeled, and I started taking the stairs two at a time.

As I jumped onto the eighteenth floor landing, I thought I heard gunshots. No . . . it was the sound of my shoes hitting the metal stairs.

Clunk, clunk, clang!

Down I raced . . . faster, faster—my breath burned my lungs in short bursts. Fifteenth floor . . . ninth floor . . . third . . . Within forty-five seconds, I swear, we had made it to the sidewalk. Adam jumped in front of a cab, threw our luggage, and me, inside, and shouted in French, "To the airport—fast."

Away we sped.

From the back window, I could see the killers touch pavement, their predatory eyes searching this way and that.

"Keep your head down, you fool." Adam threw himself on top of me in what I assume was a protective rather than amorous gesture.

Several blocks later, he let me up. "It's okay, we've lost them."

Now all the questions I'd pent up burst out of me. "Who are they?"

"Hired assassins."

"Are they after Mother and Father too?"

"Yes, but they were too late."

"Do you think—" I started to choke up at the thought of my parents being slaughtered like cattle.

"Calm yourself. I'm sure they got away. Your father is a man of many resources."

"But why—"

He put a finger to my lips, silencing me. Then he nodded in the direction of the cab driver. "We'll talk later."

CHAPTER 3

Me, Myself, and Amanda Jones

At the airport, Adam had the driver drop us at Aeroflot ticketing.

"We're going to Russia?" I asked.

"Don't be silly. The Russian mafia would sell us out for a pack of cigarettes. Here." He handed me one of the suitcases.

"I'm not carrying this."

"Fine, then leave it. They're your clothes." He turned and began walking across the terminal floor—without me!

"Wait up." I grabbed the bag and dragged it all the way to the Swissair counter.

Adam pulled me into a corner chair and handed me a passport. "Your new name is Amanda Jones."

"What?"

"You're English."

"My teeth aren't that crooked."

"Pay attention, Amanda. This is no game."

An image popped into my mind of the terrorist with the jagged scar below his left eye. That quieted me.

"Go on," I said, biting my thumbnail.

"You're flying to America to finish high school. I'm your Uncle Bob. Your parents were killed in a car crash."

I could feel tears coming, but I fought them back. (I told you, I'm not a wuss.)

He handed me a box tied with a ribbon. "Take this, go into the women's bathroom, and dye your hair."

"I'm not going into a public—"

The words froze in my throat. A huge man in a full-length black leather coat strode toward us. He had a wild gleam in his eyes. Was this the end? Was I going to die in an airport, holding a bottle of L'Oréal Superior Preference Fade Resistant Colorant Dark Auburn 4R?

At the last minute, the man swerved aside and scooped a little boy into his arms.

"Papa!" the boy squealed.

With great relief, I turned to Adam. Neither his expression nor the smooth tone of his voice wavered. He had nerve, I'll give him that.

"Don't call attention to yourself, and speak to no one. Our plane departs in fifty minutes. If you hurry, we'll just have enough time to clear customs."

I must have taken a stupid pill or something, because all I could do was gawk at him.

"Go!" he hissed. "Before they pick up our trail."

I shot to my feet like a jack-in-the-box and scooted off toward the bathroom.

English? That's what kept thrumming inside my head. How can I be English, I hate soccer . . . though I can imitate the accent perfectly since my mother *is* a Brit. Cheers.

Twenty-five minutes later, I emerged from the bathroom, a brand-new bottle redhead. The job had been easy, since, well, okay, I admit I've colored my hair before. I must say, I looked smashing. The only disturbance had been a woman in a NATO uniform who came in to splash water on her face and looked somewhat askance at the teenage girl by the adjoining sink coloring her locks. She sniffed, but said nothing.

"Come on," Adam said, dragging me to the security gate.

(How typically male. Not a word of praise for my new hair. Would it have killed him to say: "Looks good on you, Mandy." Hey, I just realized that's what every-one's going to call me from now on—Mandy! Could you just barf?)

We passed through security in a breeze, and when the officer opened my bag, I grabbed a spare pair of panties and pulled them on right then and there. (I'd thrown the wet ones away in the bathroom, of course.) Both Adam, I mean Uncle Bob, and the officer gave me funny looks.

"Much better." Smiling sweetly, I walked past them like the queen of Siberia.

Next thing I knew, we were on the plane. I sat in first class, naturally, and got a rude shock when Adam pushed me toward the rear. We were about to take a ten-hour flight in coach! Can you imagine?

"Stewardess, bring me a bottle of champagne—Dom Perignon would be nice."

Her name tag read: EVA. Her eyes were as empty as a church on New Year's Eve.

"Ve don't serve champagne, except in first kless," she said in a thick Austrian accent. "I vill bring you wine cooler, inshtead."

Adam waved her off. "We won't be having any alcohol, thanks anyway."

I freaked. If I had to sit through ten hours of tedium

with a hangover and two hundred gross, smelly people crammed around me like sardines, I was definitely going to need a drink.

"Yes, we will!" The murder vibes shooting from my eyes must have done the trick. Adam ordered two wine coolers. I drank both, and passed out.

When I awoke, we were in Omaha, Nebraska.

CHAPTER 4

Me, Back in the U.S.A.

In European circles, it is fashionable to trash the U.S.A.: Americans are vulgar, their movies dreadful, they think too much about money, they have no culture (fast food and television), and they're way too powerful. All of which is true, of course. So what? I was born on Long Island and lived there until my father's business necessitated a relocation to Geneva eight years ago. I am an American, and proud of it; so pish-tosh to the America haters, I say. The fact is: New York, Las Vegas, Miami are fun places with lots of cute boys, clubs that stay open all night, and plenty of people to look the other way if certain underage partygoers were to get carried away and, say . . . smash the twirling glass disco ball with a water balloon. (The crowd scattered like cockroaches. It made all the papers. And the owner didn't mind a bit when I said the magic words, "I'll pay.")

Even California is okay. I once snogged (kissed) a rising young movie actor at a studio party launching his newest picture, some nonsense about zombies.

Speaking of the undead . . . have you ever seen Nebraska? It's like Dante's first circle of hell. Nothing but miles and miles of flat wheat and cornfields and highways and gas stations, and then all of a sudden a town pops up and you drive through and see a bunch of dreadful, dim people wearing blue jeans and straw hats or baseball caps with stupid names on them—usually of an animal, like: BLUEBIRDS or RED GOPHERS. (Puh-leeze!)

Oh, and by the way, did I mention I witnessed this purgatory on earth through the window of a Greyhound bus? Do you know what the inside of one of those rolling garbage cans smells like? Never, and I mean *ever*, will I ride inside a bus again! The man sitting in front of us blew his nose on his shirtsleeve—twice! Total freak show. Adam didn't seem to mind at all, explaining we had to travel by bus because we needed to conserve our money. I said I would almost rather die than live like a poor person.

"Almost?"

I think I could really learn to hate that man.

. . .

After what seemed like years of trekking through featureless terrain and scorching-hot hick towns, we arrived at our destination. A tattered sign above the post office read: WAHOO, NEBRASKA. To think we were only a few miles from Venice . . . Nebraska. Joy.

"Are you hungry?" Adam asked.

Standing outside a country diner named Kitty's, the dust from the street swirled around my head and up my nose every time a truck passed. My throat felt dryer than the Gobi Desert, my tongue thicker than a gecko's. The sun throbbed like a tanning bed stuck on HIGH. What month was this? August? When I tried to answer, it came out like: "Yeth." And I don't even want to think about what the humidity was doing to my hair. (Can you say frizz?) When I caught a glimpse of my reflection in the dirty window, all I could picture was Bride of Frankenstein.

Into Kitty's Diner we went, dragging our luggage behind.

It was totally yuck. Stout, noisy men stuffed their faces with piles and piles of potatoes and greasy brown "meatloaf surprise"—whatever that is.

We sat in a booth at the back, and the waitress—a buck-toothed, moon-faced girl—flumped over to take our order. Well, my order, since Adam had gone to purchase a local newspaper. The nervous tremors throughout my body had finally begun to subside.

"Welcome to Wahoo. My name's Noreen and I'll be your waitress. You wanna know what the specials are, hon?" she inquired in a voice that seemed to come straight from her nose.

"Isn't all the food special in here?" I asked, unable to resist.

"Yeah, but I'd watch out for the liver and onions if I was you."

Mercifully, you are not me. (Don't worry. I *thought* this. I didn't *say* it.)

I ordered a buttered croissant and fruit, which I hoped would help settle my stomach, and, of course, a plate of nasty liver and onions for good ole Uncle Bob. That should fix him. Ha!

What arrived ten minutes later was not a croissant and fresh fruit but a cornbread muffin and stewed prunes.

Before I could protest, Adam returned in an altogether inappropriate good mood. "Think I found us a house, Amanda."

"No kiddin'," Noreen interrupted. "I figgered you was new in town. Where ya from?"

"England," Adam said. "The English countryside actually, near Kent."

"Where ya gonna be stayin'?"

"We are not in the habit of discussing our private business with the help," I replied. (People have to know their place.)

Her skin turned as red as a country tomato, and she stomped off.

Adam was not pleased with my effort. "This is a small town, Vict—I mean Amanda. We are going to have to get along with these people. When you behave like a horse's ass, you make it impossible for them to accept you."

"Listen, *Uncle,* don't you think it's more important that I accept them?"

He shook his head and tucked into the liver with gusto. (I hope he gets an ulcer.)

At the end of this feast, we called a cab and drove off to see our new home.

It was four miles from the center of town to an assortment of ranch-type houses on a street named Deer Lake. I could see neither. Why do people name places deceitfully? Rome is called the eternal city, but every time I've been there it's falling apart. Paris is for lovers. Wrong. There are more hateful people in the so-called city of lights than anywhere I know. Don't get me started on false advertising. Pet peeve.

We pulled up a dirt driveway toward a white-washed clapboard house, past rows and rows of tomato vines clinging to wooden crosses. A floppy-eared mutt greeted us as we knocked on the front door. A hand-made sign below the mailbox read: *THE HENNIGANS*.

"Hello. You must be Bob. Did'ja find it all right?"

The lady behind the screen door was friendly enough, lots of warmth in the smile, red cheeks, smooth skin, hair pulled back in a ponytail. The overall impression was of vigorous good health. She was drying wet hands on a well-worn apron. "I'm Connie. You'll have to forgive me, I was peeling potatoes for supper."

(Potatoes. I get it. Everybody eats potatoes here.)

"Thank you for seeing us on such short notice," Adam said. "This is my niece, Amanda."

"You're gonna be a big hit with the boys at Wahoo High." She pumped my dry hand with her damp one. "Mills? Mills?" she yelled.

A freckle-faced girl with deep blue eyes appeared from the back of the house, putting her arm around Connie's waist.

"This is Millicent, my daughter. She's a junior this year, just like you." The woman glanced at her progeny with obvious pride.

I found it corny.

"Say hello to Amanda and her uncle Bob. They're thinking about renting the guest quarters."

"Hey," Millicent said with no enthusiasm.

I caught her staring at my shoes. Was she an idiot?

A minute later, we were all standing in the middle of the main room of the guesthouse. It was blue gingham heaven (Hell?). Blue gingham curtains, blue gingham couch, blue gingham tablecloth—Dorothy in *The Wizard of Oz* might have been at home here, but I certainly wasn't.

"The bedrooms are off the living room. Each has its own bathroom, but there's no kitchen. You have to come into the main house for that, but of course you're welcome, day or night. The rent's five hundred a month plus security, and you can move in right away. What do you think, Bob?"

I glanced sideways and caught Millicent giving me the once-over, so I shot her my best "don't even think about it" look, and she turned away.

Imagine my surprise when Adam counted ten 100-dollar bills into Connie's hand.

"It's absolutely delightful, and if you'll have us, we'd be happy to stay."

What? We were actually going to live in this rusticated shack?

"Um, Uncle Bob, we have to talk," I said.

"Oh, sure." Connie smiled. "Mills and I will be in the main house."

At least she was quick on the uptake.

"Are you insane?" I asked Adam once they'd gone. "It's a two-bedroom hovel surrounded by tomatoes and rednecks with no kitchen and no servants! No, thank you. Forget it."

For a long time he stared at his hands.

"You still don't understand, do you?"

"Don't patronize me."

"There is an army of assassins turning over every rock in Europe looking for you, so they can get at your father. They're not stupid, Amanda."

"I hate that name, by the way."

"Your mother chose it, and don't change the subject." His modulated voice was beginning to grind. "Sooner or later, they'll start looking in America— that's why we're not in New York or Boston. We're in the middle of nowhere with less than thirty-five hundred dollars left, and we still have to buy a car."

"You don't expect me to believe that. Last night at the casino I won twenty-one thousand dollars."

"No, you didn't. Victoria Julianne Van Wyck won that money. It's on account for her. Any attempt on

32

your part to get at it will put these guys on our tail so fast you won't have time to paint your nails before they begin cutting your fingers and toes off one by one."

My stomach did flip-flops. "All right, you made your point."

"I'm the lucky one. Me they'll just kill, but you—"

I think I shuddered. "Stop it!" I screamed.

He closed his eyes and took a breath. I took one too.

"This is no joke. School starts here in two weeks. Try to stay out of trouble, blend in, play nice."

"Boring."

"But necessary." He almost smiled. "Which room do you want?"

"The one with the sauna and maid service."

He didn't laugh. (See, no sense of humor.)

"Pick one and unpack. Tomorrow we start looking for jobs."

(Jobs?)

He walked out, and I slumped onto the gingham couch.

I can honestly tell you I am not among the sorority of sob sisters who cry when a fingernail breaks or a pet canary gets eaten by the cat next door—good riddance, I say. But when the reality of my situation sank in, I broke down. You can laugh if you want, but I cried

33

until I couldn't cry anymore. Boo hoo. Woe is me. You would too if someone took your life and kicked it to the gutter.

What I didn't know then, but found out later, was that mousy little Millicent had snuck back and heard every word from outside the open window.

CHAPTER 5

Me, Bored

The next morning, loud knocking awakened me from a strange dream. Wild hogs were chasing teen idol Hilary Duff through a wheat field. She was wearing a duck suit and shouting, "Quack. Quack." (I love my twisted imagination.)

"Amanda? Rise and shine."

"What time is it?" I gurgled, unable to open my eyes.

"Six-forty-five. I've errands to run; I thought you might like to come along." It was Adam, outside my door.

"Think again." I pulled a pillow over my head.

At ten-thirty, I awoke for real and shambled into my tiny bathroom. Guess what I saw? Gingham wallpaper, with tiny horse paintings tacked everywhere.

The wooden toilet seat had hairline cracks throughout and was cold, but clean. The blue-and-white vinyl shower curtain appeared new, and featured cartoon seashells and daisies.

(So, to summarize for those of you taking notes—décor: horses . . . seashells . . . flowers! Kindergarten, anyone?)

The shower ran hot, then warm, then cool, but I got through it, dressed, and walked into our "cozy" living room at shortly after eleven.

"Hello?"

No answer.

It was eerily quiet. I suppose I'm used to cities. In Europe, one always detects an audible pulse. Here, not even the wind stirred. I looked out the front door toward the back of the main house. There were few signs of human activity; even doggie snoozed under the gnarled pear tree by the porch, one of my shoes nestled between its blissfully clenched teeth.

It was the first day of my new life. I stood for a long time, thinking about options. I had two. I could curl up in a ball and collapse in a lump of self-pity (not my style) or I could try to turn this mountain of lemons fate had dumped on me into lemonade. (Make that lemon sorbet; I hate lemonade.)

What did I do to deserve this?

I needed caffeine.

The kitchen was deserted. Dishes in the sink indicated breakfast had already been cooked and eaten—none left for poor Victoria, imagine.

The coffee pot I found easily enough, but where were the beans? After a bit of rummaging, I discovered the pantry.

Ta da! And just as in a *Martha Stewart Living* magazine, everything—soup to nuts—was stored in glass mason jars. (Quaint, no?) I located the electric grinder. After a few tries of too much water, not enough coffee, and vice versa, I sat down to enjoy my morning jolt. Half a muffin still sat inside the toaster oven, and the refrigerator yielded scrumptious homemade strawberry jam. I was in middle-class nirvana.

Appetite satisfied. Time to explore the house.

"Hello? Anybody home? Mrs. Hennigan? Millicent?" I knocked on their bedroom doors before entering. I'm not a thief, and I generally look down upon people who steal from others, but snooping around inside Mills's room felt more like espionage.

Her walls were covered with posters: country-western stars, American sports figures, high school banners—GO BULLDOGS—photographs, old stuffed animals, and other treasures of a teen girl's sanctuary.

In the corner opposite the four-poster bed stood an

old roll-top desk. This was the room's focal point. An aging computer, notepads, pencils, Sharpies, and reference books indicated a serious intent to study. A small bookshelf contained a cheap encyclopedia set, thesaurus, a well-thumbed Webster's dictionary, almanac, *Bartlett's Quotations,* and a portfolio of American history texts from Washington to Bush. I rifled the desk drawers but found only a few notebooks, old bookmarks, and an abandoned diary.

Dear Diary,

Mrs. Cranston is the worst teacher in school!!! She gave me a B on my Susan B. Anthony essay, which EVERYONE else thought was FABULOUS. I don't hope she dies, but I wouldn't mind a little cancer.

A Hammond map of the U.S. clung to the wall above the desk. Five blue stars dotted the topography—one in California, four on the East Coast. A name was carefully inked in beside each star. Stanford, Wellesley, Princeton, Sarah Lawrence, and Vassar. So, Mills had Ivy League ambition . . . interesting.

I closed the door as I exited.

Her mother's room was just as utilitarian, right down to the calendar on the wall filled with activities.

A work schedule showed that Connie toiled at two jobs: mornings at someplace called Kroger Bakery, and weekends at the Hormel Plant (whatever that was).

So in this, brave new beehive world, they would be the worker bees, Adam warrior drone, and I (naturally) would be queen.

Two hours of further exploration left me bored silly. I tried the television but the remote had so many buttons, it kept switching off or producing white static. (Or worse, soap operas. Ugh.) This was serious—I needed something to occupy my mind. Bookshelves in the main room contained *Reader's Digest* condensations, and scads and scads of paperbacks like Ellery Queen or Barbara Taylor Bradford. ("Her lips trembled with mad desire in anticipation of his brutish touch." Page five . . . I swear!)

I settled upon John Grisham and waded in.

Around page one hundred, I snapped the book closed, jumped from the couch, ran into Mills's room, and flung open the top drawer of her desk. You know, the human mind amazes me. I had seen it in my earlier search, but it simply didn't register. Then something— a passage from the book, perhaps—pricked my subconscious and there it was.

On top of one of Mills's notebooks lay a thin handmade bookmark. On it were written the words: VICTORIA JULIANNE VAN WYCK! No one in this town was supposed to know that name. My, my, but it's a wicked world. My mind scrolled through the possible explanations. . . .

The sound of a car pulling into the drive startled me into action. I closed the drawer, dashed out of Mills's room, grabbed the Grisham book, and sprinted to the front door.

It was only Adam, emerging from a battered green Ford Taurus.

I pushed open the screen door. "Nice car. Did you lose a bet or something?"

He didn't look pleased to see me. "What are you doing?"

"Going out of my mind with Midwest angst?"

"No, I mean, in their house. What are you doing?"

"We live here, remember? It was your near genius idea."

He came to the door and motioned me outside. "No. We live in the guesthouse out back. Don't get above yourself."

(How could anyone not "get above themselves" in this hovel?)

"She said we could use the kitchen."

"The kitchen, yes, not the rest of the house. Knowing you, you've probably already cased their rooms. You didn't touch anything, did you?"

Had he seen me through the window?

"No," I said, covering my turtle-timid retreat.

"Good. Come along, we'll get you a driver's license." He opened the Taurus's front door. It groaned.

"I'm not driving around in that heap. Someone might see me."

"Then you can walk, Miss Priss."

He started the car and gunned the engine. It actually *sounded* okay.

"I'm gonna count to three," he yelled above the roar. "One . . ."

"All right, all right." I jumped into the backseat—beige interior, worn but clean, by which I mean, no cooties I could see. I suppose it would have to do—for now.

Adam put his arm on the headrest, then turned to face me. "Aren't you forgetting something, Your Highness?"

(Your Highness?)

I thought for a moment. "Oh. Nearly forgot." I buckled my seat belt . . . nice of him to remind me.

"No, Amanda. I'm not a chauffer. From now on, you ride in the front, next to your Uncle Bob. Get it?"

41

"You're joking," I said.

His eyes narrowed, his jawline hardened. I knew that look; I'd seen it dozens of times before. He was *not* joking. Our circumstances may have changed, my whole world turned inside out, but Adam was the same old grinch.

"Fine," I snapped.

When I climbed into the front seat, he handed me a pamphlet labeled DMV NEBRASKA. "Better study. You have to take a test to earn a license in this state."

I leafed through the driver's manual, which read like a handicapped comic book.

What is the total stopping distance when the vehicle is traveling at 35 miles per hour?

a)	35 feet
b)	70 feet
c)	101 feet
d)	150 feet

The correct answer is "c." Fancy that. (Said another way, who cares?) After a minute, I finished my assignment and threw the pamphlet onto the seat. (What I was really thinking about was my name on a piece of paper in Mills's desk. Should I tell Adam? Not yet.)

"They're gonna test you on the information in

there. You'd better know it, because if you fail, I'm not bringing you back."

"Have you taken the test?" I asked.

"This morning. Here's my Nebraska driver's license." He showed me a white plastic card with his smug mug emblazoned thereon.

"If you passed, how hard can it be?" I picked up the pamphlet and thumbed through it once more, just to be sure.

The DMV building, a hideous gray rectangle, squatted on the northern edge of town. The parking lot was not full, but inside, it felt more crowded than a Calcutta breadline. We took a number, then sat on plastic seats, wedged between—guess what—still more dull people!

When my number came up, I flashed my "new" passport. I was handed a test book with a number two lead pencil, and told to black in the square for each correct answer. Completely insipid, I know, but then so are all bureaucracies. Ten minutes later I finished, and a bored, skinny state employee wearing a string tie graded my test. I passed—yippee ty yay, as they say in Geneva. (Kidding.)

"Best brush up on your right of ways," Mr. String Tie said. Then, "Next."

The actual driving section of the exam proved more

interesting. We pulled our dilapidated vehicle up to a line at the back of the building, and Adam got out. "Can you handle this?" He grinned like a serpent. I think he expected me to fail.

"Close the door," I ordered.

The driving examiner got in. TED, the name on his ID pin read. He was young and oh-so eager. "Well, looks like I got a pretty one for a change. My name's—"

"Ted?" I said, without a trace of mockery. "Rhymes with *dead*, which is what I'll be if I don't pass this exam . . . please, please, please."

I batted my eyes, and he panted like a puppy. (Men are so predictable.)

I drove around the block—very fast—but before we pulled back into the DMV, I stopped and, using my sultry voice (the breathy one every girl keeps in reserve), I said, "Ted, could you do me a big, big favor?"

He smiled. "Sure I could."

"I'm new in town—"

"I could tell by the way you ran the yield sign. Don't worry, I won't flunk you."

I handed him two hundred dollars in Swiss francs—my last. "Could you buy me two bottles of Cristal? I'm celebrating my gold medal."

"Are you in the Olympics or something?"

"British gymnastics."

His eyes nearly popped out of his head. Every guy wants a gymnast or a cheerleader for a girlfriend— something about females with their legs apart—men are disgusting.

"What kinda money is this?" he asked.

"Francs. You can change them at the bank."

"Yeah, I suppose, but what's in it for me?"

"You'd be my first new friend, Ted." I leaned over and kissed his cheek.

His face flushed. "Sure, sure. What's your number?"

"I don't have a phone yet, silly. Give me yours and I'll call you tomorrow."

(Risky, yes, but if I was going to acclimatize, I'd need champagne—and no, I'm not an alcoholic, thank you for asking. Remember, I grew up in Europe; people drink wine or bubbly with every meal. Besides, I like the taste, and the way it makes me feel—especially around boring people, who become not so boring after a glass or two—and no, I don't like the hangovers. Satisfied?)

He produced a paper scrap from his pocket, wrote down his number, and winked.

When we arrived back at the DMV, Ted slid out of the car, and I had a brand-new Nebraska driver's license—Ms. Amanda Jones.

Adam let me drive home, which I did at top speed.

Clinging to the dash like grim death, he refused to give in to his terror, or ask me to slow down. He just glared at the road, bug-eyed. I loved making him suffer. Am I bad? Probably.

"What does a girl do around here for excitement?"

Millicent or Mills (as she preferred to be called) and I were sitting on the couch in the living room while her mom and my "uncle" made dinner.

My first home-cooked meal in potato land—bliss.

Although I had to admit, the house smelled delicious—a potpourri of fresh-baked odors—probably because Mills's mother worked at a bakery.

Mills wasn't as blank as she first appeared, and when you asked her a question, you got a straight answer. She'd been sullenly flipping back and forth between MTV, VH1, and *Jeopardy*, while I peppered her with questions about the town, her life, what to do for kicks (not that I cared particularly—this was exploratory).

"Nothin' much," she replied. "On the weekend, tip the cows, T.P. old man Nessmonger's place, race across the border and pickup some brew, get sloshed, throw up, wake up with a headache."

It sounded vaguely reminiscent of my experience at L'École Suisse, except for the cow bit.

She cut me a look. "That's what my friends do. Mostly I study."

"Border?"

"Yeah, Council Bluffs. They're not too particular about checking IDs."

"Oh." The look on my face must have been as empty as the wheat fields around us, because she followed up.

"Council Bluffs, Iowa—the state next door. Guess they don't teach much U.S. geography in England, huh?"

Was she baiting me?

"No, they're still pretty peeved about that Boston Tea Party thing."

She laughed, a rollicking giggle that shook her round shoulders.

On *Jeopardy* the answer was: "Secretary of France under Louis the Thirteenth."

"Who was Cardinal Richelieu?" I said.

Mills stopped laughing and sat up straight, her attention glued to the TV. The category: Famous R's. Alex Trebek intoned the answer, "Hitler's foreign minister during World War Two."

"Von Ribbentrop!" we said, in unison.

"The Founder of Zimbabwe."

I said, "Who was—"

She said, "Cecil Rhodes?"

Point for her. This was getting interesting.

Trebek: "One of the founding members of the school of art—"

"Renoir," I shouted.

"Shit," Mills muttered.

"American World War One flying ace."

(I had no clue.)

"Rickenbacker!" she blurted with a satisfied grin.

She had scored, so I made a joke of it. "Isn't he the popcorn guy?"

"No, that's Orville Redenbacher." She laughed. "You're funny."

Back and forth we went 'til the end of the show. I won (of course), but it was a near thing. I found myself trying to make her laugh . . . or maybe I was trying to cheer myself up. (Nothing wrong with that, is there?)

After the show, dinner was served. I must have been hungrier than I thought, since I finished a big scoop of mashed potatoes with gravy.

Throughout the meal, Mills and I kept flicking each other cautious glances. Was this a growing friendship or a rivalry? Too early to tell.

When Mills's mom suggested we take her truck and fetch some ice cream, we both jumped from the table. I hankered (a Nebraska verb) to scrutinize Ms. Millicent, free from Adam's intrusive gaze. As for Mills ... I'm not certain about her motive. Maybe she wanted to get to know me, or maybe she just wanted dessert. She was proving more difficult to read than I'd anticipated.

In the pickup, driving along darkened country roads, the smell of watering crops crept into my senses. European cities don't smell like this. They smell like metal, exhaust fumes, wine, cigarettes, and perfume. This was different, clean and fresh. The night air felt delicious on my skin.

Mills didn't say much during the drive. She wasn't what you'd call a chatterbox, but I liked that. You know how some girls, and many boys, talk constantly about nothing ... yak, yak. Not Mills. She chose her questions carefully and *listened* to my answers. I had the distinct feeling of being probed.

"Is your father away on business?" I asked, to change the subject.

"Nope. He's in heaven watching over us." She said it matter-of-factly, eyes never leaving the road.

Surreptitiously, I studied her face: high cheeks, strong jaw ... the eyes were a tad too wide, but bright and clear. Behind them lay purpose and something else, just around the edges—desperation, as if she knew the world would crush her someday.

We arrived at the DQ (Dairy Queen—it's a place that sells soft ice cream) and waited in line. The cars and trucks in front and behind us at the pickup window were filled with boys and girls our age. During the day in the bus depot and the diner, all I'd seen were adults with big bellies. The nighttime brought out the teen crowd—maybe they were vampires. I'm joking . . . I think.

HONK!

The horn went off right next to my ear, and I jumped a foot.

"Hey, Mills, been studying my buns off. I'm gonna be number one this year!" Jimmy Danforth, a shaggy-haired boy with a long face and hazel eyes had pulled alongside us and blasted his horn.

"Maybe if hell freezes over." Mills's comeback drew howls from Jimmy's seatmate, a boy named Brad White.

"Say, who's the new meat?" (Meaning me.)

"The only meat I see is between your ears," I said.

"Hey, there, Betty Boop, if I told you I loved your body, would you hold it against me?" Brad convulsed anew at his own (dim) wit.

With a scowl, Mills cut in front of them, and up to the take-out window.

We ordered chocolate sundaes for Adam and Connie, and a medium cup of cherry vanilla frozen yogurt we could split. When I reached for my purse, I realized I had only a few Euros. Yesterday I'd won twenty-one thousand dollars; today I couldn't even afford to buy ice cream. Mortifying.

"It's okay, I've got some dough." Mills grinned, and I'm pretty sure she enjoyed my embarrassment. "Now you owe me one." The smile remained, but her eyes narrowed. She meant it.

As we pulled out of the DQ lot, we heard whistles from several of the waiting cars.

"Are they whistling for you?" I asked. "And why did that bozo call me Betty Boop?"

"I don't get whistled at. I'm a brain, not a babe." Mills honked her horn at the car in front, then stomped on the gas, passing the dawdler while shouting, "Dipstick!"

She slowed almost immediately and cooled down. "I can't figure you out," she finally said, after a mile or two of silent suburban cruising. "You walk around like you're something special, but you don't act like you're pretty. Most girls it's the other way around."

(So Mills was a truth teller . . . how fresh is that? She was wrong though. I know I'm pretty. I just don't sit around looking at myself all day. Remember, "pretty" is something you put on when you need to—otherwise, cool it. That's Rule #4.)

"You make me sound like an advertisement for cheap wine."

She stared at me for a moment with indecision flickering behind her eyes. "A Betty Boop is what boys around here call a hottie."

Mills turned up the dirt drive to her house, cut the lights, accelerated, then jammed on the brakes so the truck slid/stopped just short of the wooden garage door. "Mom hates it when I do that." She grabbed the ice-cream sack and ran inside.

I was going to have to wait for another opportunity to initiate a definitive conversation. I couldn't help thinking there was more to Millicent Hennigan than met the eye.

CHAPTER 6

Me, Settling In

By my fourth day in Nebraska, I had almost resigned myself to the slow (make that tectonic) pace of life in a small town. I spent my days reading American popular fiction (I never knew there were so many gifted serial killers out there), and my nights catching up on the year's worth of sleep I'd missed. Busy work became my routine. I watched Adam doctor my school transcripts, replacing Victoria Van Wyck with Amanda Jones. He had even managed to pilfer an official Swiss Education seal. Clever. Naturally, I was curious about the origin of these documents—particularly my passport—and about Adam's role in procuring them. It gave me a chance to pepper him with questions vis-à-vis his shady dealings and his private life, about which I knew little and was mildly curious.

"How does an honest man manage to get hold of goods like these, Adam?"

He took off his glasses and rubbed his eyes. It was almost midnight in our bungalow, and the crickets outside were conducting their nocturnal concert with great gusto.

"I had your name legally changed to Amanda Jones for starters. As for the rest . . ." He held up a sample of his handiwork. "The good guys have to know what the bad guys do, and how they do it, in order to keep one step ahead."

"In other words, both sides use the same methods."

"Don't be peevish; it's beneath you."

"I'm curious, that's all."

"What you don't know won't hurt you. Go to bed." He stood, stretched, then started for the door to his bedroom.

I followed him. "Do you know a lot of criminals? Is that why my father hired you?"

He fixed me with his world-weary look. "No, but I know teen agitprop when I hear it." Then he did the weirdest thing: He chuckled. "Save your energy, Amanda. You're going to need it out here."

He closed the door in my face, having had the last word—again.

. . .

The next couple days, I registered at Wahoo High, acquired textbooks, and met several guidance counselors. Go Bulldogs! Mills turned up once and helped guide me through the process, even managing to get yours truly into the same Advanced American History class as she by telling the counselor, "It's what her dead parents would have wanted."

Imagine.

She's really quite calculating, Mills. I like that.

Adam found a job working as a something-or-other in Omaha. I turned down not one but three waitress jobs, all of which paid $3.50 per hour, in conditions Torquemada would have envied. (Spanish Inquisition—look it up.)

Adam was adamant that I get a job for two reasons. One: we needed the money, and two: it would keep me out of trouble. (*Moi?* Trouble?)

"Idle hands are the devil's tools," he intoned.

Which is nonsense. Think about it. If the devil were real, wouldn't he concentrate on busy, not idle, hands? After all, busy hands belong to powerful people: captains of industry, celebrities, politicians, etc. Successful people can inflict brutal misery on the working class. And from what I've seen, some do it with glee.

Was I just rationalizing now that we were poor?

I hated the condition I was in. This had better be temporary. I don't know if I can take much more.

That night after dinner—chicken stew with fresh-picked corn and . . . potatoes (surprise)—Adam suggested I do the dishes. (He was always doing that—volunteering me for one menial task after another. Do I *look* like a servant? No. To be fair, he was always willing to "pitch in and help," which, I suppose, was a point in his favor. I'm sure he did it to annoy me though.) Before I could make an appropriately caustic reply, Mills came to the rescue.

"I'll wash, you dry."

We made a pile of suds in the sink and played a game we invented called Rub-a-Dub-Dope—Who's Got the Soap? It was a bit childish and silly, but we giggled anyway.

Afterward, Mills extended an unexpected invitation. "Want to go bowl?"

"Love to. Ah . . . refresh my mem," (Very English, that).

"You don't know what bowling is?" Her forehead wrinkled shar-pei-like.

"I'm more the equestrian type."

She explained, and we were off. It looked like we were going to have that *tête-a-tête,* and I was looking forward to it.

. . .

Bowling, in case you don't know, is a sport requiring one to wear "special" shoes that hundreds (thousands?) of sweaty, smelly people have worn before, or you can eschew the shoes (say that five times fast) and bowl in your socks. Guess which alternative I chose? If you said sweaty, smelly used shoes, you haven't been paying attention.

Mills bowled well. She's quite athletic, almost graceful in a tomboyish way.

A group of boys from her (our) high school (go Bulldogs) cavorted next to us, forestalling any attempt at real conversation. They went out of their way to show off, posture, preen, and generally act like boors. I ignored them, except when one particularly noxious cretin asked me for my number.

"I'd rather bathe in a vat of acid than go out with you."

They fell about with laughter, cuffing, squeezing, and grabbing one another.

It's too bad Freud was Austrian; he would have had a field day with the obvious repressed, homoerotic tendency of American boys. I have attended so many court-ordered "therapy" sessions myself, I can now speak the jargon of the psychiatric community as well as they.

Transference . . . taking your own unfocused anger and

laying it on others in the form of antisocial behavior.

The first time I heard that diagnosis, I said, "What am I supposed to do, bake a cake?" Clever, I thought, but psychiatrists have even less sense of humor than Adam.

Another said, "Acting out abandonment anxiety, Victoria?"

"It's not acting if I believe it."

He frowned, and scribbled like mad in his notebook, the buffoon. But enough of my psychiatric history. Yawn.

"They're part of the football team," Mills whispered. "That's how they always behave."

The boys' increasing desperation to elicit a reaction from us only made me laugh harder. Soon Mills and I were church giggling at every grunt, groan, and male-bonding moment. They were like the monkeys in the ballroom—yapping, screeching, and scratching themselves. Honestly, I think guys must have a strong chimpanzee recessive gene. One of them, their leader—quarterback—was Adonis-like in appearance. Tall, golden-haired, blue-eyed, Vance Murdock in another setting might have been worthy of a heart palpitation or two, but here he reminded me of pictures I'd seen of Hitler youth. Today Wahoo, tomorrow the world!

When Mills and I left, our sides hurt from laughing, and guess who came out into the parking lot? Golden boy himself.

"Listen, Mills, I—the boys—don't mean anything. We've been doing two-a-days [a form of football workout], and they were just blowin' off steam. I apologize."

I was moved by his stumbling sincerity, but Mills responded coldly. "We hardly noticed," she said. "This is Amanda; she's new."

"Welcome to Wahoo." He held his hand out and smiled. Lots of teeth. "My name's Vance. Hope I didn't get off on the wrong foot."

"Amanda Jones." I put my hand in his. I felt a tiny tingle in my stomach at his touch, and quickly pulled away.

Mills and I jumped into the car.

"Y'all comin' to the first game? It's next Friday. We play Davis City. Love to see ya." He turned and bounded away like a panther.

During the ride home, I let Mills babble about the pecking order at Wahoo High. At the top were jocks and the beauty bunch—prom and homecoming queens. She spoke of them with particular contempt. "Airheads," she sniffed. Next came the real surprise: Of equal importance in the social hierarchy were the

4H-ers—the kids studying agriculture. In other words, the future farmers of America!

I must have flinched when Mills told me that, which prompted a "get over yourself" look from her.

"This is farm country, Amanda. Who do you think is gonna rate out here—Marcel Proust?"

Point taken.

The second tier featured the political wonks and the smart crowd, which included Mills, Jimmy Danforth . . . and everyone else right down to the stoners.

I told her, at my old school the only thing that counted was money. Richer was better, no matter how dreadful the human being. If you had cash (more accurately, if your family had it), you were made.

"Give you an example," I said. "One of the girls in the dorm was dating a horror show who called himself Antonio and pretended to be from Spain. He was crude, arrogant, and smelled like roadkill."

Mills laughed.

"Serious," I said. "Then, one day he gave this girl a two-carat canary-yellow diamond as payback for spitting on her in public. After that, every girl in school threw herself at him."

"Disgusting."

"Yes. I spoke to one who snogged him—"

"Snogged?"

"Kissed. 'How do you stand the aroma?' I asked her. 'I just put a little perfume under my nose and think about jewelry.'"

"Guess I'd be on the bottom of that system too," Mills said.

I felt a sudden surge of pity for her. She attempted a smile, but I knew she understood the distance between us. I fell into a reverie, imagining a bleak future for the Millicent Hennigans of the world. Even if she got her scholarship and graduated with honors—then what? An entry-level position at some dreary company, putting in sixty-hour work weeks for a junior executive like Adam York. Ugh! If I had to look forward to a future like that, I'd go mad.

"Your parents must have had a lot of money too, huh?"

Her question brought me up short. "They, ah . . . lost it. You want to drink some champagne?" I said, changing the subject.

"You got some?"

I recounted the story of Ted the driving examiner, how I persuaded him to buy the stuff for me, how we'd met behind a gas station the next day so I could pick it up, how he'd offered to come back to my "place" to help me drink it. No, thank you.

(When a man or boy takes an interest, never tell

him where you live or how to get in touch. This puts you in control—and control is good.)

"I've got two bottles hidden in my room. One of them is chilling in an icy plastic bag under the sink right now. Shall I sneak in and get it?"

Her reaction surprised me. "They just crawl all over you, don't they?"

"Pardon?" was all I could manage.

"Boys, males in general."

As we made a left onto our street, I said, "Is it the kitty's fault when the fleas bite?"

She wanted to laugh, I could tell, but stifled it. Score a point for my side.

Thirty minutes later, we sat on a blanket in an open field, drinking and enjoying the night air.

We shared the bottle, passing it back and forth like shipwreck survivors. With each sip, Millicent began to loosen up and talk about her life in the Midwest, her hopes, her dreams. . . . I found myself appreciating the matter-of-fact way she dealt (no self-pity). She possessed an almost Faustian fatalism.

"Even if I end up stuck in Nebraska after college, it's okay. At least I had the opportunity to get out—if only for a little while. Most locals are born, grow up, and die here, clueless. I'll still have an Ivy League degree and my mom. Maybe I'll teach math at the university or run for congress." She chuckled to herself, but I don't think she was kidding.

When I asked if she missed her father, she said, "There's nothing I can do about it."

(Her attitude made it even more imperative I suppress any dejection I might be feeling about my situation. Call it *noblesse oblige*.)

I lay back and gazed at the stars. They were like sparkling candy in a pool of dark chocolate. I wanted to reach up and touch. Were there girls on planets orbiting around one of them, looking up at us, and wondering if we existed?

I was about to pop the million-dollar question ("Mills, how do you know my name?"), when she said, "You don't have to lie to me."

"What . . . what do you mean?" I sputtered. Had the alcohol fogged my brain?

"I know who you are, Victoria." Her blue eyes bore into mine.

"How do you know?" I wasn't about to flinch.

"I overheard you and 'Uncle Bob' that first day. Then I Googled you . . . over a hundred items—naughty girl." Her eyes searched mine for a reaction.

I relaxed. This confirmed my deduction. I found myself, once again, admiring her honest, plain manner.

"You spied?"

"Not spied." She smiled. "Just nosy. But don't worry. Your secret is safe with me."

"Does your mother know?"

She laughed again. "Good Lord, no. Mom's the biggest blabbermouth—listen, in a small town, if you tell even one person, the whole community knows in twenty-four hours. I got burned once and learned my lesson. Someday, when you want to tell me the whole story, you will." She shook my hand, and I knew she meant it. I caught myself thinking a dozen thoughts at once, unable to voice any of them.

"So?" Mills asked. Even in the moonlight I could see her cheeks flushing with curiosity.

In a rush, I blurted my sad tale. Everything—my parents, the scar-eyed hit man, the fake passports, "Uncle Bob"—all of it.

Mills nodded, taking it in stoically. Then, I felt a surge of guilt.

"It's . . . you know, there's an element of danger to you too, I guess. I mean, what if they—"

She cut me off. "You think anyone would look for

you here, in this dump? Get real. This place is the lint in the belly button of civilization—you can't even see it on the map—end of the line, last stop. Welcome to Wahoo. Believe me, you couldn't have picked a better place to get lost."

Then she grinned, Cheshire cat–like, and winked. "Besides, compared to the stuff that goes on around here, I think your life is terribly romantic . . . international scandal, secret identities, running from—" She stopped, glanced at her watch, then shot to her feet. "Omigod. It's midnight. I've gotta get home. Mom'll have a conniption fit." She snatched the blanket from beneath me, and took off running.

"Wait," I said, scampering after.

When we arrived at the house, Mills eased in through the side door. "Don't let the bedbugs bite," she whispered.

I stood for a long while, trying to get my thoughts in order. I knew she would keep our secret. I knew something else as well—I liked her.

As I slipped into the guesthouse, it felt like sneaking back into the dorm after curfew. *Plus ça change, plus c'est la même chose.* (Nothing ever changes.)

Unfortunately, Adam was still awake. He was sitting in the living room, reading *Les Misérables*. How appropriate. He was, after all, my Javert. I decided upon a lighthearted approach. "Isn't it past your bedtime?"

He closed the book. No smile. I thought I'd been rather witty.

"I don't care what time you come in, as long as I know where you are—in case of trouble, I mean."

That sounded promising, avuncular even.

"Two things," he continued. "Don't corrupt Millicent, I beg you. She's working toward a scholarship, which she and her mother desperately—"

"I know that."

"Please allow me the courtesy of finishing my sentence. When you introduce her to your dissolute lifestyle, it creates roadblocks to her success."

I knew what dissolute meant, I just had never applied it to my life choices. "I'm sure I don't know what you mean." I tried to stare him down, but he snapped to his feet, eyes blazing.

"There's alcohol on your breath, Amanda. That poor girl has to be at work early in the morning, or did you know that too?"

Okay, he had me on that one.

"Point number two, you must get a job for reasons we already discussed. It's not negotiable. Do I make myself clear?"

His manner was so hateful, I wanted to strike him.

"Why do you always assume the worst? You are projecting like mad."

"That psychobabble doesn't work with me."

"Maybe you should try analysis, Adam. I think you have a lot of intimacy issues."

The flare of his nostrils told me I'd scored with that observation. He turned on his heel. "Goodnight."

The door to his room didn't slam exactly, but it closed with a definite purpose.

"Sweet dreams, Uncle Bob."

CHAPTER 7

Me, Working?

I'd set the alarm for 5:45 just to cheese Adam off.

When I stumbled into the main house kitchen in my Vera Wang pajamas, both Mills and her mom were up and bustling about.

"G'mornin', Amanda. How are you today?" Connie beamed.

How can anyone be so cheerful at 5:45 AM?

I think I mumbled, "Fine," and plopped into one of the maple chairs. The room smelled of fresh-baked bread.

"Hey," Mills said, looking as bad as I felt.

"Hi," I answered, feeling somewhat better after seeing her.

"I don't have to be at the plant 'til seven. Would

you two stargazers like me to fix you some eggs?"

Stargazers? How'd she know about that?

After two cups of coffee and the most delicious ham omelet I'd ever eaten, the throb in my head had quieted. "That was a five-star omelet, Mrs. Hennigan."

She smiled. Her mouth curled at the corners when she smiled, just like Mills's. "Have some more."

"Ma! Don't force." Mills turned to me. "Mothers in this town show their love with food. That's why everybody's dieting."

"Not true," Connie protested. "Care for another muffin, dear?"

We laughed. Mills hugged her mom affectionately. I felt a twinge of . . . what? Envy.

A memory floated into my head . . . first year at L'École Suisse. I'd been expelled for locking a teacher in a closet. When I arrived at our villa, Mother was just pulling on her coat to leave.

"Sit," she'd said.

Picking up the phone in the foyer, she dialed, then listened. "This is Mrs. Van Wyck. I must speak to the school administrator." She inspected her nails while I sat watching every move.

"Ah, good," she responded to the voice on the

phone, "then you know who I am. What I want," she continued, "is for the man to be fired. Honestly, how does one allow oneself to be locked into a closet by a nine-year-old girl. Is this what you would call 'care-taking?' "

She listened for a few seconds, and smiled. "Excellent. Your apology is accepted. I'll send her back tomorrow, and you may expect a generous contribution to the faculty pension fund. Good day."

She hung up and turned to me, handing over a piece of paper. "This is Doctor Wurffel's address, dear. [My first shrink.] He wants to have a little chat with you. [More like stomp around inside my brain.] The driver will see you there and back, and afterwards Mumsie'll take us both for a nice supper. Good-bye, dear." She kissed my forehead and swept out the front door. The point of my story is *not* self-pity; it's that there are different kinds of love. . . .

"By the way, Amanda, Bob tells me you're not having much luck finding a job." Connie's voice broke in upon my reverie.

"Er, yes, that's right." (Did I just say "er"?)

"How'd you like to work at the library?"

"The library?" I repeated, feeling doltish.

"My boss's daughter works there, and she's leaving

tomorrow for Australia. The pay's not much, but you can read all you want."

I looked at Mills, who nodded yes.

Me, a librarian. Hmm, better than being a waitress. In fact, it might even be tolerable.

"Thank you, Mrs. Hennigan. I'll look into it."

At eight-thirty, Adam dropped me off in front of the public library at the southwest corner of the town square.

"How will you get home?" he asked.

"Don't worry about me. I'm wicked, remember?"

The head librarian was a middle-aged woman with laughing eyes. She looked forty but acted younger, as though the energy in her body threatened to burst through her skin at any moment. (If she were a book it would be titled: *Skateboarding at Midlife* or *Climbing Everest During Menopause*.)

"I'm Mrs. Brath. What can I do for you?"

"My name is Amanda. I'm new here—from England. My uncle and I are staying at the Hennigans'. Connie, that is, Mrs. Hennigan, suggested I see you about a position before the start of the school year."

"What part of England?" She spoke with an English lilt.

(Uh-oh.)

"Countryside. Near Kent."

"Small world . . . small world." Her gaze sharpened. "Your accent is difficult to place. Kent, you say?"

"I've been traveling for the past year—Belgium, Spain . . ." I flashed my winning smile.

"That bloody Spanish diphthong will ruin a good English accent every time," she said.

Her smile was even brighter than mine. "When can you start?"

"Today?"

"How's your Dewey?" Her eyes bored into me.

"Pardon?"

"Dewey Decimal System. It's the librarian's compass."

"I'm a bit rusty," I lied. I knew diddly about Dewey.

"Triple zero to one hundred is the Library and Information section—just there." She pointed. "Several texts on the subject—must remember to buy capers on the way home—then, of course, you'll want to read about Melvil Dewey himself—some books about him in Social Sciences—the three hundreds, to be exact. What did I do with my glasses?" The words tumbled out of her, one thought piling on the other.

"The inventor?" I guessed.

She nodded. "Let's see—ah—there's an excellent

biography in the History section, right around nine twenty-five, if memory serves."

I stood like a lawn ornament. Why wouldn't my brain work? Finally . . . "Yes, ma'am. I'll jump—"

Before I could finish, Mrs. Brath disappeared into the rows of books behind the checkout desk.

My very first job. Librarian's assistant. You're not going to believe it, but I was thrilled. Maybe I'm a geek at heart.

I found the nine hundred section without too much trouble, and sure enough, at nine twenty-five, there it sat: a faded blue book titled *Melvil Dewey and His System*.

I read until noon, got my very own library card, and checked out both the bio and a text called *Learning the Dewey Decimal System*. See how conscientious I am?

Outside, storm clouds had gathered . . . and I was without money or a car. Mmm . . . what to do? (Find a boy who has a car, silly. Haven't you learned anything?)

Across the square stood a hot dog place called Sizzle 'n' Franks, where several potential targets loitered. Three boys—all wearing red baseball caps with the initials STL and a picture of a bird—sat wolfing down lunch under a large umbrella. When I strolled by, two things happened. It began to rain, and they stopped chewing. One of them stared so intently at my breasts, I actually felt embarrassed for him.

A word here about gawkers. Every girl (woman) wants to be appreciated by boys (men). But the *right* kind of men, please. Not guys with mustard stains plastered all over their shirts.

I was about to give this guy a piece of my mind . . . how he'd just blown a chance to give me a ride home, when who should appear but Vance. Hunka, hunka, burnin' love.

"Hey, good lookin'. What's cookin'?" His smile was like a postcard from Hawaii. There was something appealing about his boy-next-door openness.

"I could use a ride home." I smiled back but showed no teeth. (Rule #5: Never be obvious with boys.)

"Sure thing. This here's Skeeter. He's nobody's genius, but he is one heck of a runnin' back." Vance gestured to a six-foot slab with bull shoulders, no neck, and a block head that looked as though it'd been carved from granite. "Skeeter, this is Amanda, the new girl."

So Vance had remembered my name.

"Hey," Skeeter mumbled.

We ran through the rain to Vance's pickup and piled inside. I had never scrunched between two boys with this many muscles before. European boys are softer, generally.

Vive la différence!

"Aren't you supposed to be sweating and grunting somewhere?" I asked.

"No practice today. Coach went to a funeral."

Skeeter grunted.

During the ten-minute drive, Vance attempted to convince me that he wasn't just a "jock" by engaging me in a literary discussion. What were my favorite novels? (Stendhal's *The Red and the Black,* Dreiser's *Sister Carrie.*) Had I read Rilke's poems? (Yes. German mysticism—gag.) Still, he was definitely scoring points until he said: "You know, Mandy, I read *The Fountainhead* from cover to cover—twice!"

We arrived at the Hennigans' just as the rain let up.

Vance pulled into the driveway and stopped. "Listen, what are you doin' next Saturday?"

"Working at the library."

Skeeter slid out, and I followed.

"Too bad. How 'bout a little kiss for the ride?" Vance said.

There was that smile again. I imagine it had worked its magic on quite a few local girls.

"Okay," I said, then kissed a surprised Skeeter full on the lips.

(Rule #1: Always keep them guessing.)

I ran inside, the sound of Vance's laughter ringing in my ears.

Maybe I was going to have some fun in Wahoo after all.

CHAPTER 8

Me in School

The next ten days passed more or less uneventfully. I trudged through my daily activities with as much enthusiasm as I could muster, but increasingly, I found my thoughts returning to my old life in Switzerland. I missed color. Switzerland in the summer is every shade of green. And the wildflowers are better than any florist shop. In the winter, there's blue in the depths of all that mountain snow. Nebraska is flat and brown . . . and drab. I also missed Stella and her hell-raising ways, our curfew escapades, outthinking school authorities, and all the boys I'd taunted. One night I woke at two in the morning feeling so lonely I reached for the phone and started to dial Stella's cell. Only an image of the scar-eyed assassin brought me to my senses. I crawled back into bed and willed myself to sleep.

. . .

The library became my salvation. The job itself was actually fun, and I used the last breath of summer reading everything I could get my hands on and learning the Dewey System. Sounds boring, but it wasn't.

Mills and I settled into a kind of easy companionship. I watched her spend hour after hour at the library researching arcane and complicated subjects to prepare for her SATs.

"Where can I find the collected works of G.W. Leibniz?" she inquired one Saturday.

"Who?"

"Leibniz. The guy with Isaac Newton who developed calculus . . . you have heard of Sir Isaac Newton?"

I liked it when she needled me good-naturedly. (At least I think it was good-natured. Am I just naïve?)

Vance turned up once or twice at the library to ask me out for a soda, but I kept him at arm's length. (Because I didn't need a boyfriend right then, and because anyone as good-looking as Vance needs to be brought down a peg or two.)

Mills quizzed me about my relationship with him.

"What do you talk about?"

"He talks about how Ayn Rand would have made a crackerjack football coach; I talk about French pastry."

"Is he as big an egomaniac as people think?"

"Probably."

"Has he kissed you yet?"

"No. I kissed Skeeter though—just to cheese him off."

We laughed at that.

"Why do all the hunks think they're God's gift?" she added.

Mrs. Brath was a delight. Half den mother, half nutty professor, she alternately encouraged and tut-tutted.

One day my curiosity got the better of me. "Mrs. Brath, when we first met and I said I was from Kent, you said 'small world.'"

She smiled. "Indeed I did."

"For what reason, may I ask?"

"Because my husband was born in Kent."

"Are you still together?" (Pushy, aren't I?)

"Certainly," she replied, as if I were daft to have wondered.

"Then why come all the way to Wahoo, Nebraska?"

"Same reason as you," she said with a twinkle in her eye.

That stopped me.

"To broaden our horizons, dear girl."

"Oh," I offered.

"He's an electrical engineer. Works for Tri-State Energy, out of Lincoln. We shall have to have you for tea some time. Now if you're done quizzing me, I suggest we get back to work."

Cheeky.

There was also the matter of Adam, whose job kept him busy, but not so far removed he couldn't check on me daily. He'd adopted my father's habit of referring to me as "you."

"How are you settling in?"

"Fine, within certain obvious limits."

"How's the library?"

"Stimulating."

"Do you have any problems worth repeating?"

"I'm thinking of starting a counterfeit ring."

"Euros or dollars?" he asked.

Did he just make a joke?

I have noticed in him lately a tendency to relax a bit more. Sometimes he even smiles—a tight, rubber band grin that loosens up when he's around Connie. She's only six years older and quite attractive, so I suppose romance is not an impossibility. (?)(!) On the other hand, dark circles have begun to form under his eyes—an outward sign of hidden turbulence perhaps?

Over the weekend, I even saw him lose his temper. I had just returned home from the library and was gazing halfheartedly out the window as he struggled to change a tire in the front yard. Apparently the lug wrench—if that's what it's called—slipped, causing him to scrape his knuckles.

"Son of a bitch," he yelled, tossing the tool away. After sucking on his hand a few seconds, he retrieved the wrench and went silently back to work.

I think Adam York is way more intense than he lets on.

An hour later, he came inside. "By the way, you'll need a new wardrobe for school." He handed me six fifty-dollar bills.

"Three hundred? That won't even get me a good pair of shoes."

"It'll have to do."

That Sunday, Mills took me to the holy grail of retail mediocrity—a place called Wal-Mart—which is a poor man's version of Harrods, London.

Their "juniors" section was—in a word—awful. Polyester everywhere, garish colors, no designer names (unless you consider Mary-Kate and Ashley designers); they even sold plastic shoes!

I managed to find a few natural fabrics and bought basic mix 'n' match outfits: skirts, tops, jeans. (Fashion tip: accessorize with color, a belt, or jewelry—junk jewelry in this case—which the store seemed to specialize in. Oh, and some scarves . . . the more colorful the better. Around the head, neck, or waist—fabulous.

I could see why someone might like shopping here; for three hundred bucks you can get thirty items. At Harrods, three hundred doesn't get you past the candy counter.

Mills, of course, has no taste.

She picked out one hideous top after another, all with manufacturers' names on the front—Nike, Guess, Adidas. . . .

Enough! After a severe talking to, she put them all back.

"Mills! You're not going to buy *that,* are you?"

"Why not?"

"Because the logo on the buns makes your butt look like a canned ham."

(While I'm on the subject—why do people buy clothes that turn them into walking billboards? If you're going to advertise for someone, *make them pay for it!* Except Chanel, who, as you know, is my personal deity.)

September 2.

The first day of school—nervous time. I hadn't been to an American school since I was nine, when my family moved from New York to Geneva. In Switzerland, the teachers would be skittish about dealing with me, but this was different. I was on their turf.

Adam drove Mills and me in and gave each of us a wildflower for luck. (Cornball.) Mills gushed. She's such a sucker for attention.

L'École Suisse and Wahoo High were as different as crème brûlée and Cream of Wheat.

Example: L'École Suisse's halls were lined with plush Persian carpets. Wahoo: gray linoleum. L'École Suisse: hand-carved wood inlaid lockers. Wahoo: dingy gray metal. L'École Suisse: dining room with tablecloths, china, crystal, engraved silverware, and one of the best chefs in Europe. Wahoo: smelly gym that doubled as a cafeteria, cardboard trays that doubled as plates, plastic "sporks" (spoon/fork hybrid), and "cooks" who reheated food brought in daily (monthly?) from district kitchens.

HELP!

As I said, Mills and I had one class together, AP American History, fourth period. Otherwise, I was on my own . . . terra incognito. On my way to homeroom, I got a rude awakening.

A wrinkled little man stopped me with a scowl. "Your skirt is too short."

"Too short for whom?" I sneered as I breezed past him.

He caught up like an Energizer Bunny. "I'm the vice principal here, young lady, and the dress code is strictly enforced. What is your name?"

"Amanda Jones. It occurs to me that in order to comment on the length of my skirt, you had to have been looking at my legs. Naughty boy."

His eyes bulged, he gasped, and the breath whooshed from his body. It was electrifying. His hand spasmed—I thought he was about to explode—when, once again, Vance and the footballers came to my rescue.

"Hey, there, Mandy . . . Mr. Wilbury, what's the problemo?"

Wilbury stiffened. (Mills was right about that pecking order thing.)

"S-Skirt length violation," he sputtered.

Vance chilled him with a shake of his head. "She's new here, sir, from England." He emphasized the last word as if it were a disease. "We should make allowances; after all, they're our allies."

Wilbury turned to me. "You'll find a copy of the dress code in your student guide. I suggest you read it." The bell rang, and Vance hustled me into class. We shared the same homeroom, and the thought crossed my mind that Vance might have arranged it. . . . Interesting.

We sat next to each other during orientation while the teacher droned, "Do not give your locker combination to anyone, as any illegal contraband, drugs, or weapons found in your locker during random searches will be considered your sole responsibility and punishment meted out accordingly."

Vance kept passing me Post-it notes containing his version of Shakespearean sonnets.

Should I compare you to a summer day?

You're so much prettier . . .

A sharp glance from the teacher put an end to Poetry Corner.

I was struck by the contrast between the relaxed, informal attitude of this school and the old-world formality of L'École Suisse—the way American students dressed and sat, the way they interrupted teachers' lectures on the flimsiest of pretenses.

"Excuse me, Mrs. J., but can I be excused to go to the nurse? I got a real bad pain." It was one of Vance's football buddies.

Titters all around. "Anyone sick enough to miss my class will also have to miss football practice and the game this Friday."

"Never mind," Jocko said, sitting down to jeers and applause.

Why is it called "high" school, when standards are so low?

After homeroom, Vance insisted on walking me to my next class. "If they see you're my friend, nobody will mess with you. Besides, I wouldn't want you to get lost."

His attention was flattering, and I felt almost giddy as I walked beside him. Take it slow, I warned myself.

The subject was French IV, and I soon discovered I spoke the language better than the teacher. She stopped calling on me, so as to better exercise her pedestrian talent on the other students whose command was even more feeble than her own. That didn't prevent her shooting occasional dagger/envy looks in my direction. Oh well. *On y soit qui mal y pense!* (What you wish on others comes back to you.)

Biology and Algebra II followed, and neither class looked very promising. (Who am I kidding? Algebra II . . . dial 911!) My lab partner in Biology was none other than Noreen from the diner—the nosy waitress.

I'm not sure if she recognized me, but her reaction upon finding me her seatmate was decidedly frosty. "Keep your stuff on your side, and I'll keep mine on th'other."

When lunchtime arrived, Mills and I met in the gym/cafeteria, as we'd agreed earlier.

The lines were long, the service dreadful, and the ambiance Kafkaesque. Clearly, the place had been modeled after a penitentiary—barred windows, institutional green paint, grungy floor—barf!

"I can't eat this," I said when we finally found a seat. "My plate looks like a Jackson Pollock."

"I'd rather eat an oil painting than cafeteria food," she replied. "Look at those beans—they're still moving!"

We laughed and shuddered.

"In Europe, students bring catered meals to school."

"Don't even think about it," she said. "Brown baggin' is for dweebs and geeks."

"But I'm hungry."

"Here." She pulled a shiny red apple from her purse. "Always bring a piece of fruit to tide you over. That way you'll look cool and vegetarian instead of dorky." She cut the apple in two and offered me half.

While we nibbled, she talked about her class

schedule with enthusiasm. It's easy to see why Milli-cent is an A student. She enjoys the regimen.

". . . and I was a little worried about Calculus, but I got Mr. Kaplan, who likes me, so that's a load off, and the other classes look to be a breeze, not that I'm taking anything for granted, just keeping my nose to the grindstone—pass the salt, please—and my eyes on the prize."

That's the way Mills talked when she got excited, a string of run-on sentences, peppered with a soupçon of clichéd aphorisms.

We left the cafeteria together, headed for American History, just as Vance, Skeeter, and several of the foot-ball boys entered.

"Hey there, sweet stuff. How's lunch?"

"Try the beans," I said with a perfectly straight face.

After school, Mills and I walked out together past the baseball fields, then said our good-byes. She turned east toward her job in the market; I turned west for the four-block walk to the library.

Only eight more months to go. Then . . . what?

CHAPTER 9

A Nasty Encounter (with Me)

The first week crawled by without too many bumps.

"Miss Jones, this is your third tardy in as many days. Are you trying for a school record?" It was my Bio teacher—a flinty spinster named (honest) Ms. Chips.

"What is the record?" I replied, smiling innocently.

By this time, Noreen had moved to another desk, leaving me alone with frog guts and salamander entrails. She had acquired a new lab partner, Darla, who had more facial hair than van Gogh, and was about as attractive. The two kept asking for more creatures to dissect; I suspected they were secretly snacking on them.

Mills and I lunched together daily, and in History she continually surprised me (and the teacher) with the depth of her knowledge. Not that I'm catty and competitive (*moi?*), but I decided to dig in, hunker down, and strap it on, as Mills might have put it. In other words, I studied like mad to keep up. The library was a big help. Here's a Victoria fun fact: You can find out about almost anything in a good library. (You see, though I'm naturally brainy and clever, I'm still willing to learn. You may adore me now.)

Friday came, and in the cafeteria, Vance asked me to be his date at the football game.

"Did you quit the team?"

"Haven't you been reading the newspaper? I'm the star! Next year, hell, I'll be at some big-time football college on a full-boat scholarship."

"But if you're playing the game, how can you be my date? Wouldn't that be rude?"

This knocked Mr. Quarterback off his stride, but he struggled on. "I mean, like, after the game. There'll be tons of cool parties."

"Okay," I said, "if Mills can come along too."

Now it was Mills's turn to clutch. "Amanda—" she tried.

"Sure, why not. I'll fix you up with Skeeter. See you there."

As Vance sauntered away, Mills poked me under the table. "What'd you do that for?"

"Don't you like parties?" I asked. It's an old trick

politicians and lawyers use—answer a question with a question.

Question: What time is it?

Answer: Don't you have a watch?

There are a million variations. Purists call this sophistry. I call it keeping the edge.

My guess was Millicent hadn't been on a date in eons—not that she's unattractive. It's just that some people don't think about the opposite sex, so they dress, walk, and talk as if they were, well, sexless. This is good for A students and brain surgeons, but it's buzz kill for anyone with a libido.

She was going on this date. I was determined. "Look, it'll be fun. And if it isn't, we'll break into the library and study all night."

Her eyes actually brightened at the prospect.

"I'm kidding, you toad."

First step—makeover party!

You can throw a makeover party for yourself—it's mad fun and does wonders to cure split ends, a breakup, or any other mild depression. It's even better when you do it to a friend.

Makeover parties fall into two categories. The "I think she's looking too fabulous; let's get her to cut her perfect hair into a bob." (This happens more than you know.)

The second kind is where you have a genuine concern for making someone look better, plus you get to eliminate something the other person has or does that you hate.

In Millicent's case there was a long list, beginning with her fingernails.

In the first place, she didn't have any. Mills was a classic nail biter—bad kitty—since, apart from the face, hands get noticed next most often. (I know, I know. Boys look at breasts first, second, and third—but that doesn't count. Boys aren't really people—see chimpanzee reference.) Also, your hands are generally what make initial contact with others, except in France and Hollywood, where everyone feels compelled to kiss perfect strangers on the cheek—a custom I find revolting and pretentious. I'm not kissing a stranger's face! Even if they've won the Nobel Prize—"Hello, I'm Dr. Leakey and I've just returned from disease-infested Angola." *Kiss. Kiss.*

Puh-leeze!

As my mother used to say: "First contact, first impression. Always keep your hands soft and clean, your nails polished."

When I shared this wisdom with Mills, she examined her hands, then showed me the stumps proudly. "They're clean!"

"What about the jagged nails, goofy?" I replied, perhaps a tad bluntly.

At the local drugstore, I selected a pale rose polish for her. Rule of thumb—always colorize nails to complement wardrobe, which in turn, complements skin and hair color—you wouldn't wear blue nails with a yellow blouse, and you wouldn't wear either if you had red hair.

We also bought makeup, a nail file, cotton balls, polish remover, and a top coat.

I was astonished at how little these items cost—lipstick, three bucks. At Versace, lipstick is fifty dollars!

"Why don't we just glue some of these on?" Mills had wandered into the fake nails section like a navigator lost around the Cape of No Hope.

"Drop it!" I smacked her wrist, and the packet clattered to the floor.

"W-What's wrong with you?" she stammered.

"The only people who use press-on nails are hookers and drag queens."

She understood instantly.

Next step was hair and makeup. Diana Vreeland (late editor of *Vogue*) said that hair is a woman's crowning glory. Millicent's was more like a bad wig.

"Do you have a blower?"

She thought a long time. (If you have to think about

whether you own a blow dryer, put this book down and go buy one right now!) Mills retreated to a storage closet and pulled out a Conair 550 (dinosaur), but it would have to do.

A few streaks, tips, and highlights later, hope emerged. Her hair now had shape, lightness, and texture.

"I look so girly-girl," she squeaked.

Fancy that, I thought.

Next was makeup, of which she had a rudimentary understanding. The idea is to keep it simple and basic. (Unless you're going to a Goth party. And why would you do that?)

Where I lent insight was lips. Repeat after me: Luscious lips make boys want to kiss.

I bought her Mystic Pink and encouraged her to embellish. Always finish with gloss.

Clothes and shoes were last. As we went through her closet, I put together one outfit that had possibilities . . . pink fitted top, black capris, and strappy sandals.

Then I got the biggest surprise of all.

"I . . . I have a Wonderbra," she said.

(It's moments like these that make me believe in the existence of a higher power. Music. Bells. Hallelujah!)

• • •

At dinner that night, Adam and Connie were properly appreciative of my Cinderella-esque efforts.

"Honey, you look . . . so . . . different," Connie said.

"What does that mean?" Mills's eyes narrowed.

"It means you look cool, kitty cat," Connie replied.

Everybody laughed, even Adam.

Mills and I decided to drive the Taurus. Though beat up, it was in better shape than the Hennigan pickup.

As we were leaving, Adam pulled me aside. "Midnight or close to it, okay? Remember, you've both got work tomorrow."

Party pooper.

The football game was mind-numbing. Mills and I sat on the Wahoo side of the field, making rude jokes in front of the cheerleaders, who, in my unbiased opinion, made fools of themselves.

"Two, four, six, eight—who do we appreciate? Bull-dogs! Yay!" they yelled.

"I get it. It's poetry," I yelled back. "Not very good, though."

Students around us snickered.

The two semi-clever senior cheer co-captains were Misty and Dawn. I suppose they could be considered cute—if you squinted really hard. Mills explained they were wildly popular—destined to be homecoming and/or prom queens. I hated them instantly.

"Hooray for Vance, Vance, Vance, he's the man. Hooray for Vance, he's our man. Yay!"

At one point, near the end of the contest, Vance threw the ball into the air, and something good happened (judging from the crowd's reaction). As he ran to the sideline, Misty threw herself into his arms and kissed him . . . the little tramp.

Mills chortled. "So, the ice maiden has a heart after all. You're jealous."

Don't you hate it when one of your friends tries to nail you with an "insight" that is totally wrong? First: I'm not the jealous type—especially not of prom queens/cheerleaders—puh-leeze! How vacant can you be? Second: I am not an ice maiden. Definitely. I have feelings; I just don't wear them on my chest like a stupid letter sweater. I decided to pout.

After the game, we met Vance and Skeeter by the gym and piled into an enormous Cadillac SUV. It was clearly Vance's father's car, but Vance insisted on calling it "his baby."

We drove to a hamburger stand, where local teens congregated, ordered four burgers to go, and sped off toward my first party in Wahoo.

Mills and Skeeter sat in the darkened backseat, not saying much. She seemed so tiny next to him.

Vance tried to get me to slide closer. "C'mon, Mandy, you have to help me eat these fries. That's it, dip 'em in the ketchup and put 'em in my mouth."

(I know what you're thinking: Did I play this silly game with him? Yes . . . until he licked my finger.)

"You're on your own now," I said, sliding away.

Skeeter snickered and snorfled.

"Shudup," Vance snapped.

I caught a whiff of alcohol on his breath.

We arrived at a party inside someone's suburban ranch house, and stayed exactly three minutes. I'll explain.

It was what they called a "breakout/make-out."

The boys broke out the alcohol, everything from vodka—Vance's favorite—to Jägermeister, a sickening sweet brew invented, no doubt, by Lucretia Borgia.

Skeeter chugged half a pint the second we stepped into the party house, then screamed, "Look at me. I'm a Ty-ran-a-sore-*ass*! Wahoo!" He grabbed Mills and slow-danced into the crowd. The expression on her face was pure bewilderment.

"Ever had vodka and Dr Pepper?" Vance asked.

"Not in this lifetime," I said. "Isn't there any champagne?"

"This is a liquor party, darlin'. Wine is fine, but liquor's quicker." He preened at his hokey rhyme, then offered me a shot.

"You go ahead. Think I'll mingle."

I wormed my way through the crowd of slow-dancing bodies, Vance trailing behind.

All of a sudden, the lights went out. I felt a pair of hands grab me, followed by a rough kiss on the lips, and a brutal squeeze of my breast. "You've been teasing me long enough," someone hissed, squeezing even more fiercely. I pulled away and punched as hard as I could. I didn't see my target, but the blow hit home. I could tell by the squish on my knuckle.

"You little bitch!" It was Vance.

I pulled free and ducked between two couples. Sheryl Crow blasted from the speakers. *". . . The first cut is the deepest."* Pitch dark—disorientation—but I was able to feel my way through the crush and out the front door. Guess who was standing there sniffling and clutching her torn blouse. Mills.

"That bastard," was all she said, but I knew what had happened.

"Let's get out of here."

We ran down the crowded driveway and out to the side street. A glance back revealed the lights were still out.

"I can't believe I was actually looking forward to this. My first in-crowd party. . . ." Mills looked defeated.

I felt miserable. After all, it had been my idea. "Vance got me too, but I hit him. How far from home are we?"

"Five miles, maybe six. But we're only a mile and a half from the main drag. We could hitch."

"Hitchhike?" (I'd never done that before.) "I'm game," I said, and off we went.

Neither of us said much. Occasionally Mills cursed and rubbed her chest, but she didn't cry. After fifteen minutes or so of walking a dark country road under a crescent moon, we spotted headlights coming toward us from the direction of the party.

"Behind that bush. Hurry!" Mills whispered.

We ducked into the growth beside the road and waited. Closer and closer the headlights came. I felt like an escaped convict hiding from the hounds.

As the huge car passed, we could see Vance and Skeeter inside. Vance was holding a beer can to his right eye.

When the taillights disappeared from view, I yelled, "Wait 'til my uncle finds out!" (Who was I kidding?)

"Shh." Mills tapped my shoulder.

We resumed the trek in silence, our shoes crunching the gravel beneath our feet.

"I don't know if we should tell anyone about this," Mills said at last.

"You want them to get away with it?"

She looked past me without answering.

"I'm no prude, but I have no doubt what would have happened if we'd been too drunk to defend ourselves—someone's got to stop them."

"Look, Amanda, you don't know how things are." She turned to me. "In a small town, if you take sides against local heroes, you're asking for trouble—and that's the last thing I need right now. Besides, Vance's father is one of the richest men in the county. You don't go up against a family like that. It'd be their word versus ours." Her voice quavered but didn't crack. She had obviously made up her mind.

(I was about to press the argument, when it struck me. How many times had I gotten away with toxic behavior simply because of my family's wealth? It started me thinking, I can tell you, and I'm not the hand-wringing type.)

"Okay, fine," I said.

Another ten minutes of hard walking, spurred on by the dread of another close encounter with the football "heroes," and we arrived at a gas station.

"Lordy, look who's getting gas," Mills squealed.

I half expected to see the creeps. Instead, Mills broke into a trot, shouting, "Jimmy! Jimmy!"

It was Jimmy Danforth, the second smartest kid in school, pumping high octane into a restored Mercury coupe.

He smiled at Mills. Thank God. My feet were killing me. High heels. I coulda kissed him. I didn't. Don't get excited.

"Sure thing. I'll take you home. What are you two doin' out here with no car anyway?"

"It's a long story," I said, pushing Mills into the front seat, while I climbed into the back.

"What are you dolled up for, Mills? You look hot."

She covered her ripped blouse with her jacket.

"Jimmy, I don't want you to think I'm not grateful for the ride, but I just don't feel like talking right now."

He blinked twice, then nodded. "Whatever you say."

Jimmy drove on in silence to the school parking lot, where I picked up the Taurus.

"Stay put, Mills; I'll follow you home in my car."

At the house, Jimmy hopped out and opened Mills's door for her. "Feel better," he said before he drove away.

"He really likes you."

"I'm going to bed." She sighed, then let herself in

through the side door. I saw the lonely little reading light go on in her bedroom.

It was only ten-thirty.

I felt depressed right down to my toes. Because of me, this honest, hardworking girl had suffered a deep humiliation. . . .

I'm sure some people might say, What's the big deal about an unwanted grope? Right? Wrong. So wrong! If you don't draw the line, then there are no boundaries, and people like Vance and Skeeter can do whatever they want, whenever they choose.

And to think, I had set up this date. Plus, I'd gotten Mills's hopes up with the makeover. I remembered how her eyes glittered as she paraded for her mother. I felt low.

I walked to the back of the house amid the sound of chirping crickets. A light was on in the kitchen. Adam and Connie were cozily sipping coffee and yakking about . . . what?

Tiptoeing to the side of the screen door, I leaned against the bricks, being careful to stay out of sight. They spoke in low voices, difficult to make out at first, but my ears soon became attuned. (I have fantastic hearing. I should probably be a detective. Kidding.)

Connie: "[muffled] The problem with Mills is getting her to lighten up. I worry she'll burn herself out.

She told me once [inaudible] . . . didn't want a vacation because that would set her back a week. Can you believe it? Care for another slice of pie, Bob?"

Uncle Bob: "I'm stuffed. I wouldn't spend [inaudible] worrying about Millicent. She's too grounded to hurt herself. Hell, I admire her drive; that's what it takes to get ahead. Besides, you're one to talk, Connie—two jobs and a teenage daughter to take care of."

Connie: "[laughs] keeps me outta trouble."

Uncle Bob: "Where do you see yourself in ten years?"

Connie: "Me? Oh, I don't know. Here, probably—with Mills and her kids."

Uncle Bob: "Ever thought about remarrying?"

Connie: "[inaudible] . . . don't think so. It just feels . . . too soon."

Uncle Bob: "[inaudible]"

Connie: "What about you? Ever been married?"

Uncle Bob: "Who'd marry a self-centered workaholic like me?"

Connie: "Don't sell yourself short. You're what folks around here would call a catch."

They were flirting like mad. (Barf.) I did not need this. I was about to ease away, when I heard—

Connie: "Where do you and Amanda see yourself in ten years?"

Uncle Bob: "Not together, that's for sure."

Connie: "Why?"

Uncle Bob: "She hates me."

Connie: "No! [inaudible] . . . she's bright, poised . . . terribly mature . . . self-possessed, is what I'm trying to say."

Uncle Bob: "That's the problem. Amanda doesn't care about anyone but herself. When she discovers she's not the center of the universe, it's going to be a helluva shock."

Connie: "[inaudible]"

I'd heard enough. I darted around the far side of the house.

CHAPTER 10

Me and Mills

"Mills," I whispered, tapping on her windowpane.

The crickets stopped chirping, as if to eavesdrop.

Mills pulled aside the curtain. She was wiping her eyes.

"Let me in," I said.

"It's late."

I knew she was miserable. "Please," I said.

She looked at me for a long moment; then: "Use the side door."

I didn't plan what I would say as I slipped into her room. Surprising, since I'm usually more calculating.

"I'm okay." She sniffed.

I sat on the bed and blurted, "When I was fifteen, I was nearly date-raped."

She whirled in her chair, knocking the phone off the desk.

CLANG.

"What . . . what happened?"

"Sophomore year, I snuck out of the dorm after curfew with a friend. Her boyfriend was older—eighteen, I think—and he brought his cousin along.

"We drove to a private hunting preserve, parked, and began drinking and telling ghost stories. It all seemed innocent enough."

"Go on," Mills said, handing me a piece of watermelon sugarless gum. (I hate gum, but I popped it into my mouth anyway.)

"After a while, I had to pee, but I was scared to go out in the woods alone, so my date offered to come along as a bodyguard. We walked some ways down the trail, and I hid behind a tree. Well, no sooner had I pulled my panties down than lover boy was on me. I remember the feel of his cold hands on my thighs. I fought him, scratched his face, bit, kicked—but he threw me down, knocking the wind from my lungs. I lay there gasping for air, the weight of his body almost causing me to black out, the smell of rancid breath blowing in my face. I thought I was a goner, when all of a sudden, a look of horror came over him, and he leapt to his feet." I paused to blow a bubble.

Mills's eyes glistened with anticipation. "Well, what happened?"

"A family of wolves had encircled us, probably attracted by the struggle. Not ten feet away. Terrifying. The biggest wolf—undoubtedly the alpha male—bared its fangs at my would-be-rapist, causing him to run away like a child.

"I got to my feet, ready to bolt, but the wolves turned and melted into the night. One remained. A silvery female trotted over, her coat luminescent in the moonlight, but before I could be scared, she licked my hand, as if to let me know I'd be all right. It was magical. Then, she ran away.

"We got back to the dorm safely. I never saw the boy again, and I've never told another soul until now."

Mills leaned against her desk, blinking like an owl. "Is that true?"

"Not a word. I don't even know if there are wolves in Switzerland. I just wanted to cheer you up."

"You bitch!" She laughed and spritzed me with a bottle of water.

I laughed too. I love telling that story. The point is, if you believe something is protecting you, maybe it is. Who's to say your guardian angel isn't a big, bad she-wolf? Okay?

. . .

We spent the next hour or so talking about life, boys, love, and other mysteries. We didn't even need champagne to sustain the good feeling. Imagine that.

At midnight, I eased out the side door, sneaking into the guesthouse unobserved. Adam and Connie, looking way too chummy, were still gabbing in the kitchen.

I washed the makeup from my face, slid into bed, and fell asleep the moment I turned out the light.

CHAPTER 11

Me, Bonding

The alarm went off at 7:00 AM, and I awoke with a vague feeling of unease. My bedroom was cold; storm clouds had gathered outside. Pulling on my robe, I peeked into Adam's room. He was sleeping, snoring softly, so I hurried into the kitchen to see if I could catch Mills—too late. Connie sat sipping from her cup and staring at the newspaper, but not really reading. The smell of fresh coffee and homemade cinnamon buns filled my nostrils.

"G'morning, Amanda. Need a cuppa joe?"

Need? "No, thank you. A spot of tea, perhaps."

As I headed for the cupboard, Connie touched the back of my hand. "I try to respect my daughter's privacy . . ."

I put the kettle on the boil. (If I ignore her, will she go away?)

"But I know something upset her last night."

(Uh-oh. Any conversation with an adult that features the word *upset* is not one you want to be part of.)

"Mmm," was all I said.

She plowed onward. "When I asked Millicent about it, all she'd say was that you and she got through it together." Tears appeared in the corner of Connie Hennigan's eyes. Then she hugged me. "I do love my daughter . . . thank you."

Normally this would be a yuck moment for me, but she so obviously meant it, I let her clutch for a second or two.

"We'll be fine," I said, pulling free. "It's all part of the weather report for teen girls: serious aggravation followed by a smattering of pain and heartache continuing on through adulthood."

She laughed. I think it was relief more than my wit.

"I've got a couple minutes before I have to leave. Why don't you get dressed and I'll make your tea."

"Umm." (Be careful about letting grown-ups do you favors, no matter how well intentioned. Key word—*reciprocity*. They'll want that favor back someday. Danger.)

"Green or black?"

"Black, but you really don't have to—"

"I insist." Her smile was practically beatific.

Not knowing what else to say, and not wanting to encourage any more "heartfelt" conversation, I waited for the tea, then walked out.

Saturday morning at the library, Mrs. Brath was all in a tizzy—restocking day. That's when new books arrived from the New York publishing houses and got painstakingly integrated into the Dewey system. Some of the older inventory then got remaindered—wait, am I babbling?

Anyway, shortly before lunch, something odd occurred. While we—library staff—hovered around the shelves like a gaggle of hummingbirds, I noticed two senior girls from my homeroom whispering, giggling, and pointing—at me! "Pay no attention to the foolish" is not only my motto, it should be a law. So I ignored them.

Several minutes later, two other girls joined the coven, cackling so loudly, Mrs. Brath confronted them.

"If you insist on jabbering, I shall have to ask you to leave. This is a public library, not a sorority party."

The four exited en masse, with many whisperings and backward glances aimed at yours truly.

These girls were obviously having some fun over

me. Why? Do I care? No. Just damned annoying is all. The rest of the day passed without incident, and by nightfall, we'd finished our restocking chores.

"Nicely done," Mrs. Brath said. "Have a cookie."

When I got home, Mills, her mother, and Adam had dinner on the table and were waiting for me.

Mills rolled her eyes—a secret signal. Something was up.

"Here's a surprise for the two hardest-working girls in Nebraska."

"I'm going to retire," I said. Mills laughed. Adam didn't.

"No, no. I made *coq au vin*." (Chicken in wine sauce.) "Your uncle said it was your favorite." Connie opened the stew pot; the intoxicating wine/herb mixture was like a love letter from Johnny Depp. No, better. After a steady diet of meatloaf and potatoes . . . (puh-leeze).

We ate like condemned prisoners. I'm not too ashamed to say, I even licked the bones clean.

And strawberry shortcake for dessert! There is a heaven, after all.

Adam produced a Scrabble board, and we played round after round of team scrabble. Mills and I murdered them. It was clean, sadistic fun, pulverizing adults in a word game.

"What is oblates?" Connie asked.

Since it was my word, I wasn't going to give an inch. "Challenge or play."

She grabbed the dictionary. "Oblate, noun . . . ML oblatus (Latin): a child dedicated in his or her early years, by the parents, to the monastic life. Oblates."

I looked at Adam as the definition was read to see if he could appreciate the secret irony, but, as usual, his features gave no indication either way.

I did notice, at one point, that his hand brushed Connie's, reaching for a letter. She pulled away, blushing. Interesting.

I wondered if Mills saw this too.

Sunday, no work, so Mills—after several hours of studying—and I decided to catch a movie. Adam gave me the car (whoop-ti-do), so us "gals" drove to Omaha. We settled on a subtitled French movie called *The Swim*, which I found impenetrable, but Mills adored.

It was about a mystery novelist who stays at her publisher's country house and commits a murder—or is it all just one of her imagined plots?

When we left the theater, another odd thing happened. Mills spotted one of her friends across the street.

"Sandy? Sandy!" she yelled.

The girl stopped, saw Mills—clearly saw her—then

turned away and galloped down the street, dragging her mother along.

At the end of the block, Sandy said something to her mom, who then turned and gave Mills a bone-chilling look of . . . what? Anger? Disgust? It was as if someone had passed gas in a crowded elevator.

"What's that all about?" I said, sticking my tongue out at the woman.

"I don't know." Mills watched mother and daughter get into their car and drive off. "I've been in the same math tutorial with her for two years now."

"Maybe she finally realizes the hopelessness of competing with a math stud like you."

Mills didn't even crack a smile. Was I losing my touch?

On the drive home, we yakked and yakked—well, Mills mostly yakked . . . about staying on point to get her scholarship, how hard she'd worked (I knew that; I'd seen it), how important it was for both her and her mom, how her dad would be proud. . . . At one point, she stared at me with the intensity of a snake handler.

"Have you ever wanted something in your life so bad, and dedicated so much of yourself to getting it, that if you didn't, you wouldn't want to go on living?"

"Hardly," I replied. But the question got me thinking. Was anything that important to me?

I did admire Mills's commitment though, maybe even envied her passion. The popular word these days—one must have passion.

A boarding school classmate of mine used to swan about, saying: "I'm passionate about art!" and "I'm absolutely passionate about classical music."

Totally phony.

I'm passionate about clothes, but I'm no freak. (Except where shoes and purses are concerned.)

When we returned home, Mills attacked her study course—um—*passionately*.

She was determined, all right. I can truthfully say I've never seen anyone work harder than Millicent Hennigan.

CHAPTER 12

Me Versus Them

Monday morning broke cool, breezy, and way too soon. After a light breakfast—I made the toast—Mills and I got a ride to school with her mom, who gave us each a juicy pear for lunch. (Remember the cafeteria food?)

I was not looking forward to homeroom, since Vance was going to be there.

"I'm glad I don't have any classes with Skeeter," Mills said. "How do you feel about seeing 'He Who Must Not Be Named'?"

"Like Marie Antoinette before the guillotine," I replied.

Glib answer aside, I felt paranoid butterflies chasing each other inside my stomach. When Mills and I parted at the front entrance, I reached out. "Wish me luck," I said. (God, I'm needy.)

"You won't need any luck; you're good."

Wonder what she meant by that?

I walked into the classroom expecting the worst. How was Vance going to react? "Hey, baby, what happened to you?" Or would he be cool? "You missed a killer party. Too bad." Perhaps he'd go the Vin Diesel route, "Nobody slugs me and lives to tell the tale."

Instead, to my relief, he'd changed seats and now sat on the opposite side of the room, in the back row, where one of the cheerleaders fussed over his black eye! The desk beside mine was empty.

It was going to be easier than I thought. I had been violated (not for the first time) and fought back (which you must always do). In fact, I'd hit the school super-star and gotten away with it.

Vin Diesel, meet Amanda Jones—the Terminator.

Throughout homeroom, Vance and his football posse acted out, as my shrink would say, loudly cele-brating their great Friday night victory. They huffed like a herd of buffaloes, but everyone expected it of them, including the teacher, so no one paid particular attention.

When the bell rang, I was the first one out. Down the hall, I sprinted. When I turned the corner, I stopped and looked back to see if anyone (Vance) was following me. Nope. They exited as a group and walked the other way—like a blue-gold stain on a calm sea.

Fear used to give me an adrenaline rush. I remember once, on the Via Veneto in Rome, upsetting a fruit cart on a dare. The vendor chased me six blocks with a carving knife, threatening murder if he caught up, and all I could think was—what fun! Not anymore though. I must be maturing.

French class was turning into a walkover. The teacher, Mme. Breton, had given up even trying to challenge me. Embarrassing for her, no doubt, since my accent was so much more authentic than hers.

"Étudiants, attention, s'il vous plaît," she always began. Honestly, I think she is French Canadian, which, to a real Frenchman, is a little like being trailer park trash.

"Can someone give me the pluperfect for the verb 'to seek'?"

Mine was the only hand that shot up.

"No one?" she offered. (So now I'm no one. I wonder if she's channeling my father.)

Biology class proved interesting. I had had trouble getting my locker open, as gum had been jammed into it, so I was the last to arrive. Someone had poured water on my seat. So childish.

Paper towels dried the spot, and while wiping, I noticed waitress Noreen and her seatmate, Darla, flashing "gotcha" looks. I threw the towels into the trash bin near their desk and whispered to Noreen, "Love that dress. Kmart?"

Her face reddened and puffed out like one of those spiny fish that fills its body with air so as not to be eaten. Sudden thought: What'll I do if she pops?

Algebra II is harder than I thought. Definitely. I may even have to work at it. Thank God I've got Mills.

Lunchtime came, and I found myself ravenous. (Is it something in the Midwest air? Water?) In any event, I actually ate a whole portion of macaroni and beef. Imagine.

Mills watched with a mixture of curiosity and revulsion. "Weirdest thing happened," she said between bites of her Bosc pear.

"Enlighten me."

"After Calculus, I went to my locker to pick up my study guide, and found three cheerleaders waiting."

"Let me guess. Misty, Rain, and Storm?"

"Misty, Dawn, and Peggy. So I said, 'Hi. Lost again, ladies?' "

Now, I am not a giggler by nature, but Mills's bon mot made me laugh so hard, iced tea squirted from my nose.

Mills continued, "Then Dawn gets all in my face and says, 'Stay away from Skeeter.'"

"Get out," I said stupidly.

"For real."

"Your boob must have made a big impression on that country boy."

"Shut up," she said, smiling in spite of herself.

"Hey, Mills, mind if I join you?" It was Jimmy, sitting without waiting for an answer.

"Suit yourself," Mills said.

"Look what I scored." He held up the new SAT prep book from College Press.

Mills's jaw dropped, cartoon-like. "Where'd you get that?"

"Went to the University Bookstore in Lincoln over the weekend. I told you I was serious about beating you this year."

She trembled to touch it, as if it were a religious relic.

"You wanna get together and study?" Jimmy asked.

"Does a frog have a watertight butt?"

Jimmy laughed—a honking, uninhibited kind of laugh.

"My place, Wednesday night," Mills said. "Bring the book."

She talked to him flippantly, but I could tell she was

not as indifferent to his . . . charm, as she pretended. The fact is, he wasn't so bad—in a cheese-and-crackers sort of way. It was equally obvious he fancied her, and was trying hard not to show it.

"Okey-doke, Wednesday at eight." He glanced at me. "Hey, Amanda. Sorry. Didn't notice you there." He dashed from the cafeteria, like a pup with a new squeaky toy.

(Didn't notice me? That toad!)

After the final bell, out near the buses, one of the football jerks passed by, offering a greeting. "Bee-yatch!"

Less than two weeks here at good old Wahoo (go Bulldogs), and I've already found my niche—Amanda the bitch. Didn't I tell you life wasn't fair?

CHAPTER 13

Me, Harvest Queen?

I don't know when it dawned on me (honestly, I think my brain rusted in Nebraska); maybe it was the second time someone jammed gum in my locker or the third time I walked past a group in the hall and they all started coughing.

At lunch, I laid it out for Mills. "Vance and Skeeter have started a smear campaign against us."

She stopped chewing her apple, swallowed, and washed it down with a sip of milk. "I think you're right."

"I know where Vance's locker is. Shall we trash it or leave him a note warning him to back off?"

Mills thought for a moment. "We'd just be throwing gasoline on the fire. I say ignore them; it'll die down."

"Ignore them?" I think I sputtered. "My locker's

got gum all over it . . . when I show up in homeroom, I cause more coughing fits than Typhoid Mary." I actually pounded on the table. "Please don't tell me you just said *ignore* them."

The two girls sitting next to us got up and slunk away, exchanging worried glances.

"Shh," Mills said. "We're only juniors, Amanda."

"So?"

"So let's not make waves. After we graduate, we'll get some payback. Meantime . . ." She finished her milk, squashed the carton, and stood up, looking somewhat sheepish. ". . . there's nothing those jerks can do to prevent me attaining my goals. Listen, I'm . . . I'll catch you later." She spun away and walked out.

I was so P.O.'d I could hear my teeth grinding like the reverse gear in our crummy Taurus.

So that was Mills's solution—roll over and play dead. Well, not me. Not ever.

If a burglar breaks into your house, you don't give him a cookie—you set him on fire. (Okay, I realize I just used another fire reference, but it was only a metaphor, and I repeat I'm not a pyro.)

The point isn't could we take this garbage, but why should we?

Appeasement.

Bad idea. The worst.

Here's an example how appeasement works.

Last year during Christmas break, Stella and I stayed in Lucerne to catch a little extra skiing. Stella was dating one of the instructors, which didn't hurt.

It was a perfect excuse to avoid the whole holiday-with-the-family, bored-out-of-my-mind thing.

The only problem was, while staying in the dorm, you still had to obey curfew.

After about the third night, the floor monitor caught us coming in late (very late—why wasn't the little snitch asleep like she was supposed to be?).

Worse, she minicamcorded us.

Busted.

And . . . she said she wanted five hundred dollars or she would turn us in!

"F#*k off," I'd said. Stella paid.

Appeasement.

Two nights later, little Miss Blackmail came back, demanding more money . . . see what happens?

This time, I gave her a check—explaining I'd redeem it for cash the next day.

Stella called her boyfriend, Hans, got him to bring his camera, and we snuck him into our room.

Morning came; so did the floor monitor, who took the cash and returned the check while Hans recorded the scene from our closet.

When he revealed himself, Miss Blackmail fell to her knees and begged us not to expose her. She gave us back Stella's money—and mine—crawled away, and a month later, she was gone.

Don't you agree I was honor-bound to retaliate on Vance and Skeeter somehow? Time to sharpen the Van Wyck swift sword of justice. *Sic Semper Tyrannus*.

The next morning after breakfast, Mills sucked the wind right out of my sails when she handed me a greeting card with a peace symbol drawn on the front. The inside of the card read: *I'm sorry*.

When I looked up, she grabbed my hand. "I hate them too, but please, Victoria, go with me on this one little thing. I'm begging you."

We argued about it awhile, but in the end, I relented.

"Okay," was what I said.

In hindsight, I suppose I should have known better. If you don't kill the cancer, the cancer kills you.

The next few weeks passed with only a few incidents— giggling behind my back, pointing, whispers—kid stuff.

Meanwhile, Vance, Skeeter, and the other football boneheads traveled the hallways in packs, like hyenas, barking and howling at all in their path. The team was undefeated, and there was talk of a state championship, which undoubtedly fueled their testosterone-heavy arrogance.

In October, ballots came out for Harvest Queen. The usual suspects were nominated: half the cheerleaders with stripper names and . . . *me*, the only junior! Imagine. When I saw the list on the bulletin board outside the cafeteria, you could have knocked me over with a pom-pom! Amanda Jones—Harvest Queen? Mother would be . . . proud? Chagrined? Flabbergasted?

At lunch, Mills and Jimmy handed me a bouquet of wildflowers.

"Surprise!" they said, nearly causing me to choke on my fruit smoothie.

"Did you two goofballs put my name in?" I pretended to be angry so as not to gush. (I hate gushy.)

"No," Jimmy said, sounding surprised at the question.

"Cross our hearts. . . . Isn't it cool?" The smile on Mills's face was genuine. She was actually rooting for me.

"We've come up with a strategy that could win," Jimmy enthused.

"Yes," Mills continued. "We position you as the underdog candidate."

"Underdog? Moi?" I said, but she kept right on going.

"You're the standard-bearer for the unfashionable crowd. It's perfect!" She effervesced with proletarian pep.

(Victoria Julianne Van Wyck as working-class hero? Doubtful.) But before I could veto the plan, Jimmy blurted, "Besides, you're a Betty."

Mills slugged him on the shoulder. "C'mon, let's go," she said, dragging him away.

"Ow! What'd I say?"

Have I mentioned my Creative Writing class? No, because I've been saving the best for last. It's the final class of the day and is taught by a flamboyantly gay man named Huell Moore. Talk about a fish out of water, he sports silk handkerchiefs—in Wahoo! Everyone gives him a wide berth because he stands six-foot-six and has muscles bulging on top of muscles. Also, he's clever as paint, witty, and seems to want to encourage his students to write. There are only eight of us in class, so we get a lot of face time with him.

"Call me Huell," he tells us.

One day, after we'd been asked to write a one-page composition, he held me past the bell.

The assignment was: "Describe who or what you are and your life's ambition."

Everyone else had written what fell into one of two categories. Either: a) a paean to free verse that would've made Walt Whitman palpitate in his grave ("I aspire to be the wind that carries love across planet Earth. . . ."), or b) the sort of *Reader's Digest* personality condensation you'd find on the dust jacket of a Bill Gates bio ("I am persistent, determined, ambitious, and fun. Someday I hope to run my own business.").

Huell began our private meeting on a metaphorical note. "You're the pussycat that ate the canary, aren't you, Miss Amanda?"

"I'm not a fowl fancier, frankly." I thought he might enjoy an alliterative flourish.

He did, clasping his multiringed fingers together, contemplatively. "Will you read your piece to me, please?"

I took the paper from him, and cleared my throat.

"I am an island in a stormy sea to which no pirate or shipwrecked sailor may lay claim. I stand alone—me."

When I finished, he smiled. "You're going to pass this course with flying colors. All I ask is that you challenge yourself."

Before I could employ adult-speak with him, he stood and opened the door. "Write a story, say, five thousand words, about something controversial. That's your assignment for the semester. Oh, and you don't have to attend my class if you don't want to. Ta ta." He swept out of the room, silk scarf trailing in the wind.

Was he kidding? I wouldn't miss it for the world.

One Wednesday night, at the library checkout counter, three girls from my homeroom appeared.

"Excuse me," the middle one began, "do you have any books about lesbians?"

They giggled.

"Check in the Women's Studies section," I answered.

More snickers. The tall one spoke. "Shouldn't we look under *P* for *pervert*?"

Their infantile game began to annoy me. "In your case, look under *I*, for *ignoramus*."

Their faces froze into Harlequin masks.

I turned to help a father and his son, and the three skulked away.

CHAPTER 14

Rumors about Me

When I arrived at school next morning, I discovered my locker had been superglued with bits of carpet.

"Did you see who did this?" I lashed out at a group of freshman girls who happened to be walking by. "Did you?"

They darted away like a school of frightened fish.

Outside homeroom, I was gathered up by one of the hall monitors, a gangly-looking boy named Rudy, with a speech impediment. "Guidance counselor wants to see you."

"What for?" I asked.

He shrugged his shoulders. "Guidance, I guess"— the last phrase so audibly juicy, I could feel the spray all the way down my arm.

. . .

"Hello. I'm Mrs. Gray. Won't you sit down, please?" (If ever a name fit a person's appearance, it was Mrs. Gray's, from her hair to the color of her dreary office.)

She had my file spread out upon her desk.

"Miss Jones, isn't it?"

I smiled.

"Transfer student from England, correct?"

I nodded. I had decided upon the silent treatment.

"How are you settling in? Any problems so far?"

I shook my head.

She cleared her throat and squirmed. "Sometimes the adjustment can be a rocky one." She leaned across the desk, oozing concern.

I gave her my blank expression, with a hint of Mona Lisa smile, but said nothing. She was going to have to come to the point without my help.

"Just remember, if you have anything you'd like to say to me—in complete confidence, of course—on any subject, no matter how delicate . . ."

(Puh-leeze! She was beginning to sound like a shrink.)

"Don't hesitate to come see me. 'Kay?" She stood. I stood.

She held the door open for me. "You may rely on my discretion completely." Somber as a church deacon.

That was it? We were done? I hadn't said a word.

As she was closing the door, I stuck my head back inside, which startled her, judging from the flair of her nostrils. "I really enjoyed our little talk," I enthused, then closed the door.

In the empty hallway afterward, I turned a corner and spotted Mr. Wilbury, the puffy vice principal who'd accosted me on day one about my skirt length. Fate, destiny, kismet—you choose the word. I happened to be wearing the same cute little skirt that showed my legs to good advantage. (False modesty is not one of my shortcomings.)

I saw him glance at my hemline and pick up steam. At three or four paces, he began blinking behind thick glasses—surprisingly, he averted his gaze and chugged on by.

"Mr. Wilbury?" I said.

He turned a corner and sped away, pretending not to hear.

Had I suddenly acquired the power to make adults flee before me?

As I sauntered into homeroom, ten minutes late, the football crowd in the back began cough-talking, you know, where you pretend to cough but you're really saying something. The most common cough-talk word is "bullsh*t." Try saying it and disguising the sound with a cough—you'll get the idea. It's childish and obnoxious, therefore boys think it's cool.

A chorus of "like . . . like . . . like" filled the air as I strolled to my seat. Like what, I thought.

"Knock that off," the teacher said.

Silence.

"Miss Jones," she continued, "you are ten minutes—"

"Guidance counselor." I interrupted. "Here's the note."

She sneered at all of us, then returned to her blackboard, scratching agitated chalk strokes upon the helpless slate.

Question: Why would anyone want to teach high school? Adults know, or should know, most kids dislike them or, at the very least, mistrust them. So why bother?

After French class, Madame, as she liked to be called, pulled me aside. "I have a present for you."

"Merci." I unwrapped the package. A book. *Emma Bovary* by Flaubert, in the original French.

"There's really no need for you to attend this class; you're skilled enough to be teaching it."

After weeks of frigid disregard—this. Hmm.

"It simply would be a distraction for the other students and a waste of your time to continue."

Distraction?

"You will receive an A, of course, and I'm giving you a permanent pass to study hall. Your time would be more productively spent there, I imagine."

"Thank you."

Her manner was coldly dismissive as she turned and walked away.

Fancy that. Two teachers had told me not to bother with their class. Huell's was obviously more affirming. I think he wanted to help. Madame's was different, as if I'd contracted a disease requiring quarantine. Curiouser and curiouser, as Alice in Wonderland once mused.

At lunch, I sat in our usual corner table near the exit, nibbling a pear, but Mills hadn't shown. When Millicent Hennigan said she'd be someplace, or promised to do something, you could count on it—that I knew—and she'd specifically said she and Jimmy would be here to talk about the election.

Should I worry? Should I look for her? Maybe I'll just stay here and make faces at the table of girls staring at me.

That's when Mills slunk in, sat down, and handed me a note. Her eyes were red-rimmed and puffy.

"What's wrong?"

"Read it," she said.

HENNIGAN! We don't associate with lesbians or queers. Suggestion: You and your fancy-pants dyke friend transfer . . . or else.

In an instant, it all became clear to me. The stares, the vandalisms, the girls at the library, the cough-talkers. They hadn't been saying "like," they'd been saying "dyke."

Then Madame "suggesting" I not come to class, and thereby protecting her girls from . . . me? Even these morons in the cafeteria, giggling and pointing, thought Mills and I were lesbian lovers . . . it was all around school!

The absurdity of it hit me like nitrous oxide.

I laughed so loud, every one in the cafeteria stopped to gape at me.

"Shh," Mills said. "They'll think you're crazy!"

"I am crazy."

I jumped to my feet and ran to the group of girls who'd been giggling. "How stupid are you?" I said.

Their smiles froze.

"Pardon?" one said.

"You think I'm a lesbian?"

They exchanged nervous glances.

"How do lesbians act? What do they look like? Are you lesbian experts?"

Two of them stood and I swept their food trays—drinks and all—right into their laps.

"Answer me!"

All four scattered, one with a squeal. My blood pressure must have redlined as Mills pulled me from the cafeteria, into a bathroom across the hall.

"What are you doing?" she asked.

"Those people are ignorant. They wouldn't know a lesbian if it bit them. And even if we were, so what?"

"Do you want to get us expelled?"

"Of course not."

"Then calm down."

As usual, Mills's sensible solution was the correct one. The bell rang before I could argue, though I nodded in what I hoped was a reassuring manner.

"Come on, we're going to be late."

We passed two senior girls as we exited the bathroom, and they exchanged a guilty whisper.

"Cretins!" I hissed.

. . .

All through American History, I brooded. Mills was clearly upset by this slander campaign. Of course, it was obvious what had happened. Why hadn't I seen it instantly? In order to cover themselves in case we filed a complaint about their assault, Vance and Skeeter concocted a story . . . their alibi.

Mills and I were the culprits. Sapphic sirens who lured the two all-American heroes into depravity. And I'd wager there were a dozen loyal team members and their girlfriends willing to "testify" against us. Diabolical.

I was not going to take this lying down.

CHAPTER 15

Me and the Principal

"Mr. Hart doesn't usually see students without an appointment." His secretary's manner was as dry as a cornhusk.

"Tell him it's an emergency."

"What sort of emergency, dear?"

"The kind that could result in a massive lawsuit."

She was out of her chair faster than a widow at a Sadie Hawkins dance.

In mere seconds, she re-emerged from his office. "Principal Hart will see you now. Just a couple of minutes though, 'kay?"

I was through the door and into the inner sanctum in a blink. There, behind an oversized oak desk sat the great man himself, the head bulldog at Wahoo High, Principal William V. Hart.

"Sit down," he said, adjusting his rimless spectacles. "Hope you don't mind if I eat while we talk."

Now I knew how Dorothy felt upon meeting the Wizard of Oz. What a disappointment. He was small-ish, with dull eyes, more rodent than eagle, thin, and utterly unimpressive.

"Mr. Hart, a terrible injustice has been done."

"Oh?" He took a bite of his sandwich.

"My friend and I—her name is Millicent Hennigan—have been accused of being lesbian lovers by the quarterback of the football team."

"Vance?" A piece of tuna fell from his mouth and skittered down his nondescript tie.

"Yes, Vance. I don't especially mind this grotesque slander—I think it's laughable—but Mills feels ag-grieved."

"Mills?" That was the third time he answered me with a question.

"Millicent Hennigan. She's an A student, very hard-working, and . . . and as decent a person as there is." (Amazing. He knew the football quarterback, but not the smartest girl in school.)

He punched commands into his computer. I couldn't see the screen. "And your name?"

"Amanda Jones."

More computer punching. "You're a new student here . . . from England, correct?"

"Yes."

Was I going to have slay the Wicked Witch of the West and lay the broomstick at his feet before he'd help?

His brow furrowed as he scrolled through the files. "You sure it wasn't a joke—admittedly a bad one?"

"Our lockers have been vandalized."

(This was not going the way I'd imagined. He was either dense or had another agenda.)

"Do you have any proof that Vance or any of the other athletes in school were responsible?"

"No, except he's the only enemy I've got."

(An image of Noreen, Mr. Wilbury, and the three girls in the library popped into my brain. Also the French teacher—Madame. Okay, I've made more enemies than friends—so?)

"Why would Vance do something like that to someone he barely knows?"

"He knows me well enough. He took me to a party a while ago, tried to get me drunk, and grabbed my boob!"

Mr. Hart came to his feet. "Ms. Jones, I will not

tolerate profanity in this office. This is America, not England."

(What a pompous twit!)

"Are you at least going to talk with the creeps? Or would you rather I call the police?"

His face grew harder than pig iron. "I will look into the matter, Ms. Jones. Good day."

I walked out of his office and into a sea of blank faces staring at me from the hallway.

Mills and I met after the final bell. We retreated to a quiet bench, where I recounted the meeting with Hart.

"I told you, didn't I?" she said. "You can't win a fight with those people."

"I'll be buggered if you think I'm just going to roll over for them."

"Fine, stay on your high horse." She blew her nose with a big *HONK!* "I've got to go to work."

She seemed a forlorn figure walking away that day, head bowed, shoulders slumped. She acted beaten, but I wanted payback. Just because we're girls doesn't mean we can't make war. Why couldn't she see I was right? Life sucks.

That night, when Mills and her mom went to bed, I told Adam all about it.

"I thought we'd agreed you'd try to keep a low profile out here." First words from his mouth, unsympathetic as always.

"I can't believe I actually thought you might be on my side for once."

(Rule #7: Use the guilt approach whenever possible. Adults are always guilty about something—why not let it be about how horribly they treated you?)

"This is bigger than that, Amanda." He rose from his seat by the fireplace in our crummy bungalow.

I knew what was coming: another "take more responsibility speech." Puh-leeze. I have my whole life to be responsible, what's the hurry?

"You know we're all responsible for who we are," he began, "and ultimately what happens to us."

"I'm to blame because some football jerk groped me without my permission and is telling everyone I'm a lesbian?"

"You went out with him, didn't you?"

"Yes, but—"

"And knowing your taste, I suspect you knew he was a jerk to begin with. I see how you manipulate people, Amanda."

"You make a compliment sound like an insult." I turned away, bathed in dramatic tension. This is usually effective. Not today.

"I don't worry about your emotional state," he continued unfazed. "You're tough enough to take care of yourself."

(Two compliments in a row. Wow!)

"But Mills . . ." A look of real concern invaded his normally taciturn face. "Can't you see this could throw a monkey wrench into her college plans?"

"How?"

"Rumors become fact in a small town. Something like this could creep into her permanent record, then bye-bye scholarship."

"That's insane. 'Millicent Hennigan can't come to our college because she's a lesbian.' Ha! There are laws, you know."

He scowled. "Don't be obtuse. It's more subtle than that. Maybe she gets dropped from a committee or two . . . a counselor decides she's become distant or antisocial . . . she gets poor evaluations for cooperation." He stopped pacing and turned to me. "It could be any of a thousand things. Discrimination of this sort is insidious. You should know that."

For the first time in a long time, no snappy reply came to my lips. He was right, plain and simple. "What do you suggest?"

"Has she told her mother?"

"She's not that naïve."

"Good. I don't want her to worry."

His answer surprised me, I must admit.

"What then?" I asked. "Will you talk with the principal?"

"I don't put problems in the hands of petty bureaucrats—and you shouldn't either."

This conversation was getting uncomfortable. He was making way too much sense.

(Rule #2: When adults start winning an argument by force of logic, immediately change the subject.)

Before I could, he nailed the coffin shut. "Vance may require a surprise visit."

My heart actually fluttered—I swear—not so much at the words, but for the grim energy that lay behind them. More than once I had seen Adam dispatch drunken assailants. In Naples, he had even taken on one of my temporary boyfriend's Italian bodyguards, who was as big as the Coliseum. *Pow! Doink!* It was over in a flash, like a Jet Li movie, only without all the kung-fu caterwauling.

I'm not a vindictive person (perhaps a little), but the thought of Vance and Skeeter with bruised lips was lovely. "When?" I asked. "Where?" I was a tad too eager, and he knew it.

"Never mind. And don't mention a word of this to

anyone—not even Millicent. No one knows, so no one tells. *Capisce?*"

"*Prego.*" I love speaking Italian, it's so . . . unnecessary. "By the way, have you heard anything from my parents?" I don't know why that came out, but it did.

"No, and I don't expect to. Way too early." His tone never wavered, but he looked away from my inquiring gaze.

"But—," I tried.

"I mean it, Amanda; this is a dangerous time. Stay out of trouble. And don't go snooping around behind my back! Hear me?" He turned on his heel and marched into his bedroom, locking the door.

Snooping around behind my back . . . what an odd thing to say. In the three years I'd known him, he'd never expressed any interest in what I thought of him and/or his methods. Our relationship had always been one of stern guardian (him) and wayward charge (me).

This was classic old-world attitude. I'm sure that's one of the reasons Father entrusted him with the job of watching over yours truly.

Still, it was maddening. What was I supposed to do with my frustration? I had come to Adam—confided in him—and gotten a rebuke. Why? Did he have no heart? In all the time I'd known him, he rarely showed even a glimpse of an emotional life. He did smile more in Connie's presence, but, by and large, I'd have to say Mr. York transformed himself into the proto-perfect modern exec—all smooth, shiny surfaces with nothing to hold onto. So why was he all of sudden worried about me "snooping"?

I felt something tingle at the base of my skull. He was hiding something. I could feel it.

Rule #3: Never underestimate your intuition. Women posses it, just as cats can see in the dark. We need it, I think, because men can be so devious. Treat your psychic feelings like the gifts they are, and they'll serve you forever. Ignore them, and they'll wither and die.

A plan formed in my mind. It was time for action!

CHAPTER 16

Me, the Spy

The next morning, Jimmy picked up Millicent and me early. Though he knew nothing about my . . . past (Mills kept that secret), he let me borrow his car for the day on the pretext that I had errands to run in Lincoln. I dropped them at school, then drove back to the Hennigans' so I could follow Adam surreptitiously. Parking at the end of our block, I pulled a furry hat over my head, and hid my face behind the newspaper.

At 7:55 Adam pulled out of the driveway. I waited until he turned right at the corner, then put the car in gear and lurched forward. Jimmy's clutch was touchy, but I soon got the hang of it.

Adam made an unexpected left through a yellow light at Grand—I was going to lose him. I hit the gas, so Jimmy's car sped through the intersection, and a red light, with a squeal of rubber. I barely missed—talk about cliché—a white-haired lady in a minivan.

The headlines of the *Wahoo Star-Register* flashed through my imagination: SWISS HEIRESS PLOUGHS INTO OLD WOMAN. (Do you ever think stuff that is almost creepy weird, and wonder if you are cracking up? Would you admit it if you did? Yeah, right.)

I pulled over to the curb and slowed to a crawl in case Adam saw my intersection stunt in his rearview. I accelerated after a block or two and spotted the green Taurus. It was headed for the highway.

A quarter mile later, Adam veered onto the Inter-state 80 on-ramp, traveling east. I followed, four cars behind . . . perfect position.

At the downtown Omaha Central exit, he pulled off, turned right, motored straight on Central for three blocks, then veered into a four-story office building parking lot.

Since the structure wasn't too crowded, I kept my distance. On the second sublevel, he found a spot near the elevator and parked.

I eased into a space behind a cement column forty yards away, got out, and, darting behind cars, trailed him into the building.

This was the tricky part—the elevator. I peeked through a crack in the door, just in time to see elevator

#2 sliding shut. Elevator #1 was already descending from the fourth floor, therefore, I reasoned, Adam was aboard #2. The light stopped at three.

I'd have to use the stairs. Fortunately, I run like a gazelle.

Arriving at the third floor, not too badly out of breath, I peered around the corner to get my bearings. I was in luck. Across the hall from the stairwell, and down a bit, stood an office labeled: FINANCIAL INSTRU-MENTS ARBITRAGE. Adam walked inside, swinging his briefcase jauntily. Don't you hate it when men walk around like they own the planet? Self-confidence can be attractive in the opposite sex, but Donald Trump arrogance? Gag.

I pushed the door open a little farther and was about to step into the hallway, when I saw a movement that made me pull back. A man approached Adam's office . . . something familiar about him . . . the way he moved—something. At Adam's door, the man stopped and straightened his tie. I nearly gasped out loud, as in a Brontë novel where the heroine discovers the unspeakable.

It was the killer with the scar below his left eye, who'd followed us down the fire escape in Brussels.

My breath came in gulps; an electric shock shuddered through my body; even my socks felt too tight. It was the second time this man had induced panic within me.

I watched as Mr. Scar-eye smoothed his oily hair, straightened his collar, and entered.

As soon as the door closed, I dashed back down the stairs, the wind escaping my chest in loud grunts as I jumped onto each landing. Reaching the bottom, I flung open the fire door and ran into the parking structure.

Jimmy's car was gone! The spot where I'd parked it by the column was empty. In fact, most of the other cars were gone, too. Even Adam's. I felt light-headed, disoriented. Was I going to faint?

I slumped against the cement column, and the cold hardness reassured me. I took a bunch of deep breaths and soon, I'd calmed myself.

Of course, you know what happened, right? I had run down one sublevel too far. I was on three; the car was on two.

I walked up one flight, pushed through the door on level two, found Jimmy's car behind the column where I'd left it, and Adam's Taurus still sitting by the elevator.

As I jumped into Jimmy's Mercury, a scary thought darted into my mind. What if Mr. Scar-eye had parked on this level and was, even now, coming toward me. A parking garage would be the perfect place for an ambush—no witnesses. I jammed the car into gear and roared up the ramp at fifty miles an hour. Stupid.

At the entrance on Central, I had to slam on the brakes to avoid an oncoming truck.

I screamed, but skidded past without making contact.

Soon enough, I was on the freeway headed back to Wahoo. It gave me time to think. What did I know? The man I'd seen going into Adam's office was definitely Scar-eye, the thug from Brussels.

What was he doing here, in Nebraska? Coincidence? No way! Was he here to murder Adam—Omigod! No. He had paused to straighten his tie and smooth his hair. If it had been an assassination, he'd have put a mask on or at least sunglasses to conceal his identity. This was obviously some sort of business. What kind? Were he and Adam in cahoots to murder the Van Wyck family? If so, why leave me alive? And did Adam even know where my parents were hiding? Would they tell him, but not me? Perhaps. My father's confidence level in his only daughter (me) was not terribly high. (How do I feel about that? Don't ask.) Something didn't add up.

Wait . . . Adam didn't get nearly as good a look at

the killers as I did. I'd seen them in the hotel hallway, then out the back window of the cab. All Adam got was a fleeting glance from a fleeing cab in the rain.

Maybe Adam didn't know the man was a killer. Should I go back and warn him? Call the police? And tell them what?

My thoughts chased around my head so rapidly, I knew I had to stop and collect myself or I would surely crash. I pulled off Highway 80 into a truck stop called Big Junior's.

Sitting in Jimmy's car with traffic whizzing by at a million miles an hour, I remembered what one of my psychiatrists told me.

"Whenever you feel the world closing in, find the quiet place inside your mind and rest a while."

I had tried that technique a few times without much success, because, as you may have gathered, I am not a quiet, restful person by nature.

This time, I really concentrated. I needed answers. What should I do? Five minutes later, I was on Highway 80 returning to Adam's office.

Here was my reasoning. If Mr. Scar-eye was looking for Victoria, he wouldn't recognize me now. Remember, I'd dyed and re-styled my hair, put on five pounds—hey, I was too skinny before, relax—and with this hat pulled over my eyes . . .

The point is, I'd warn Adam. What would I do if Adam and the assassin were allies? Play it by ear. Improvise.

When I arrived back at the office, I purposefully pulled into sub-basement three, and parked in the corner. I walked up to two to check on Adam's car—gone!

Had he left with the killer? Had the killer abducted him and driven away? No, then the killer would have left the Taurus behind. Only one way to find out.

I opened the door to Financial Instruments Arbitrage, pretending to be a delivery girl. (Picture it.)

I'd found a notebook on the front seat of Jimmy's car, and by sheer chance (I told you I was lucky), an unopened pen box in the glove compartment. I pulled the hat low on my forehead, turned up the collar on my blouse, and affected a cold.

"At-choo!"

The receptionist averted her head. (If you ever *don't* want to be noticed, act like you're sick. People tune you out quick!)

"Delivery for Mr. Jones." *Cough, cough.*

"I'll sign for it." She couldn't have been less pleased to deal with me if I'd been Osama Bin Laden.

"Sorry, I have to deliver it to him personally."

"Mr. Jones stepped out." She sneered.

"For the day?" I asked, pushing a little.

Her annoyance level was at fever (no pun intended) pitch. Phones were ringing, I was coughing. . . .

"Just a minute!" She practically spat the words at me. I bet she feels more obliging when *she* has a cold.

I used the pause to make a covert reconnaissance of the office. The reception area was smallish and unremarkable. Two leather chairs sat opposite the receptionist's desk, glass-topped wooden tables displayed all the financial trade mags—*Forbes, Inc., Barron's.* . . .

A short hall beyond the reception area contained four doors, two on either side. Did that mean four executives? Two execs and two assistants?

"I don't know when Mr. Jones will be back. Is it important?"

I nodded, then sneezed. *At-choo!* "Wait. I suppose I could leave it on his desk."

Her relief to be rid of me was evident in the wave of her hand. "Last door on the right."

I saluted and scurried down the hall. This would have to be quick. I pushed open Adam's office door, half expecting—what? Scar-eye? I felt the fear rising inside my throat and pinched myself on the arm. Get a grip, Victoria. The room was empty, save for a desk, a few chairs, and file cabinets. The desktop was clean and well organized. (Don't you hate people who are too neat?)

I tried the drawers. Locked. The cabinets. Locked. Then, I saw it. A letter sitting in the IN box. I scanned it quickly. Did I just hear footsteps? Someone coming . . .

The letter was addressed to Siemens Reserve Bank, Cayman Islands. "As regards your recent query . . ." blah, blah "we are recommending a short position on Euros . . ." blah! Financial gobbledygook. Here's what made my eyeballs bulge. Attached to the letter was a check for $150,000, made out to Adam York, for services rendered, dated . . . today! So the Van Wyck family was poor, but dear Adam certainly wasn't.

I shot out of the office just as an older man walked through the opposite door. He never even looked at me.

At the receptionist's desk on the way out, I made one last pass. "Thanks. By the way, I was doing a delivery earlier on the second floor and saw Mr.—what's his name—the guy with the scar by his left eye?"

She glared. "I'm sure I don't know *who* you're talking about."

RING.

I was out the door before she got another good look.

CHAPTER 17

Me, Sharing

I drove back to Wahoo in the kind of Midwestern thunderstorm you see on the Weather Channel: lashing wind, rain, and lightning. It was as if the atmosphere had taken on the character of the turmoil inside my mind. I'm used to a certain amount of stress—as you know by now—but this . . . this helpless, little-girl-lost feeling . . . sickening. The adrenaline coursing through my body caused my hands to squeeze the steering wheel so hard, I thought I could feel the plastic pulverizing. I forced myself to concentrate on the road . . . watch that white line, nothing else.

I needed to talk to Mills. She would bring a different perspective to the problem, perhaps even clarity. Besides, I knew I could trust her.

(Funny thing, trust is. Just a few months ago, Mills

and I wouldn't have trusted each other sharing a licorice whip, and up until an hour ago, I'd trusted Adam with my life.)

I arrived at Wahoo High just before lunch, parked Jimmy's car in the student lot, and went directly to the cafeteria to wait for Mills. My stomach was an empty knot, since I hadn't eaten breakfast. Even the cafeteria food smelled good—meatloaf and potatoes, surprise.

Grabbing a tray, I stood in line behind two junior boys who kept shooting sidelong glances at me and pretending to cough obscenities.

"[Cough] Dyke! [cough]"

Do boys like this ever grow into real men? Doubtful. I leaned close to one of them. "If every male were like you, we'd all be lesbians." I showed him my teeth. His cheeks puckered, like in a cartoon. He dropped his empty tray and ran from the cafeteria yelling: "She's gonna kill me! Help!"

A few people laughed; mostly they looked away.

I got my food and sat in Mills's and my favorite corner to wait. She arrived a minute later, alone, face buried in a calculus text.

"Hey," she said, dumping her satchel onto the Formica dining table.

I dropped my voice to a whisper, "We have to talk."

No answer.

I reached over and pulled the book from her hands. "I said, I need to talk to you—" I felt a flash on the left side of my face. Was I shot? I jerked my head backward. There, standing beside us, holding a digital camera, stood buck-toothed Noreen and her hairy friend, Darla.

"Trouble in paradise?" Noreen sniggered.

"You two weren't gonna kiss, were you?" Darla asked.

"Shut up." Mills pushed away and ran from the cafeteria. Students all around us laughed their idiot heads off.

I'm not a violent person, but my stress levels were red-zoned. I grabbed a handful of mashed potatoes and slung them into Noreen's face. "Have some food!"

She reeled backward in shock. Darla reached out for me, but I knocked her hand away.

"Don't *ever* touch me!" I snarled.

The laughter in the room died like a bug on a mosquito zapper.

Then, I strode out as if I *were* Queen Victoria. (Mother would have been so proud.) In the hallway, I called, "Mills, wait up."

She either didn't hear me, or kept running to get away. If I chased after her, the students milling about their lockers would assume we were in the midst of a lovers' spat. (Do you see how vicious sexual rumors are?)

"There goes the new girl—lipstick lesbian—gross!"

Try to imagine walking around school with everybody whispering that behind your back while someone is plotting to kill you. I felt the bile rising in my throat.

After slipping Jimmy's car key through the slot in his locker, I eased out a back door. From the parking lot, some boy I'd never met yelled, "Queer."

I headed for the library, and since the rain had stopped, I knew I could manage it easily enough. I needed a quiet place where I could think.

"Cutting classes, I see." Mrs. Brath's doleful eyes peered down at me through bifocals. "Not a good idea."

"It's kind of an emergency," I replied, slumping into a chair beside her.

"Are you all right m'dear?"

"Fine. Could I borrow a sheet of paper, a pen, and an envelope, please?"

She reached into one of the drawers behind the counter and retrieved the stationery. Envelope and ballpoint pen followed.

"I'm afraid I won't be able to work here anymore."

She touched my arm, and I didn't mind a bit. "Why on earth not, sweetie?"

"It's . . . it's a personal matter. That's all I can say. You've been very kind." I could feel tears welling, and I forced them back.

She gazed at me for a moment with what I can only describe as warmth. "Very well, dear. If there's anything—"

"No." I knew where this was going. (Rule #6: Don't let adults get too deeply involved in your problems. It's like feeding pigeons—they'll never go away if you do.) "Thanks anyway," I said, retreating to an empty table in the Research section.

I wrote for a solid half hour, filling two pages, front and back, then sealed the envelope carefully.

I looked up to see Mrs. Brath gently ushering one of the town hobos outside. It was her habit to let the homeless loiter in the library during inclement weather.

"Rain's stopped, Mr. Nedney. May I recommend a spot of fresh air?"

As he shuffled off, I pondered the unpredictability and cruelty of fate. What had this old man done—or not done—to deserve a life filled with such misfortune?

"Mrs. Brath," I murmured, "may I have a word?"

She turned to me. At one o'clock on a school day,

the only people in the library were mothers, their toddlers, and other kidlings romping about in the children's book section.

"Of course," she answered.

"I beg you to give me your word you will not open this envelope or try to read its contents until the appointed time." I held the envelope just out of reach, like a present.

Her eyes narrowed, then focused. "You have my word. Here's your pay for the last two weeks." She handed me a check; I handed her the sealed envelope.

"Thank you, Mrs. Brath. I can't tell you how important this is." (You'll laugh, but I actually gave her a little hug before I walked out.)

At the exit, I could see her image reflected in the glass door. She was staring at the writing on the envelope that read: *To be opened in the event of my death.*

CHAPTER 18

Me—Getting to the Bottom

I cashed my check at the bank—$211.21 for two weeks' work. At this rate I'd be a self-made millionaire in only 166 years.

I caught a ride home with the mailman, who prattled about his garden and asked a dozen nosy questions, which I deflected. "Thanks for the ride," I shouted as he pulled away.

Making sure no one was home in either our cottage or the main house, I eased into Mills's room. The computer screen flashed on, and I Googled Van Wyck International. There were 12,673 entries.

I clicked onto the main Web site. There was the familiar logo—*V* and *W* inside a circle made of lightning-bolt dollar signs. The symbolism was clear enough:

Stay inside the Van Wyck circle and your money will be protected. (Sure.)

Once again, the tears tried to force their way out. I kept thinking how hard my mother and father had worked to make the company successful. The vacations they never took, the sacrifices they—

"Stop it!" I said the words out loud. "No dwelling." I hate people who dwell on their sad, pitiful lives.

The Van Wyck home page appeared onscreen. What was I looking for? Something . . . a clue . . .

Make a Trade	Investments	Brokers
Company Profile	Company Update	Employments Opps
Contact Us	Intuitional Services	Your Account

I found myself tempted to click on *Contact Us*, but I decided against it. In case you didn't know, any e-mail or Internet contact you make *can be traced*. You think you're sitting alone in your room, and how could anyone find you among millions of users? Believe it, they can—Adam told me that once.

I settled for *Company Updates* and clicked in. Nothing unusual. There was a blurb about expansion into Hong Kong, the predictable company tittle-tattle about this manager or that having a baby, or winning a local award for some charity or other, but nothing—wait. At the bottom, I spotted this:

Company founder Walter Van Wyck [Daddy!] will not address the European Investors Conference this year due to minor back surgery. Chief Financial Officer Dianne Calstrop will attend in his place.

Back Surgery? It sounded like the kind of public relations announcement (lie) they'd use to cover his disappearance. The company was still doing business . . . good. If you owed money, you'd keep going so you could pay it off. You know the kind of relief you feel when you expect to get a C on a test but it comes back a B+? That's what I felt just then.

Hope.

They would settle with the mafia, stay in business, and send for me, in time. After all, Daddy was a very clever man, and not an easy one to find or kill. Mother would be safe with him.

An image of my father appeared in my mind's eye. It was last summer . . . I'd gone to the corporate tower on my birthday for lunch. We were walking from his office across the arbitrage trading floor, where dozens of bright-eyed MBAs sat glued to their Quotron screens, watching the dance of the financial markets. I remember

Daddy had his arm around me. . . . At every desk we passed, the occupant looked up at him with some mixture of respect and admiration—and my father greeted them all with a smile or an encouragement.

"Excellent timing on the Paribas trade, Viktor."

Or, "Natalia, if you keep getting bonuses, you'll be earning more than I do."

Or, "I have the Zeiss merger papers on my desk— help yourself."

He was their leader, *pater familias*, and what they felt toward him was clearly more near love than hate. I wondered why we didn't have that kind of relationship.

Daddy, where are you when I need you most?

I said a silent prayer for my parents' safety.

My questions about Adam and Mr. Scar-eye remained. I clicked out, shut down the computer, and scribbled Mills a hasty note:

Mills, don't be mad at me. We have to talk.
Need your help.
Please, please, please.
V.

I went back to my room, locked the door, and crawled into bed. I needed to make a plan, but first, a nap to refresh my mind.

. . .

"Amanda?"

It was Mills knocking on my door. Three thirty-eight PM.

"Mumph?" I think I said.

"Open the door, 'kay?" she replied.

I pulled on jeans and a sweater, then let her inside. "You got my note?" I asked, rubbing sleep from my eyes.

"Yeah."

She seemed ill at ease with me, something she had never been, even when we first met.

"It's all over school how you went off on Noreen."

"She had it coming."

"Whatever." Mills walked into our gingham living room; I followed like a terrier. "The latest rumor is that there are pictures. . . ." Her voice dipped audibly, as though she were afraid someone else might hear. ". . . of us making out in the parking lot."

"Pay no attention to—"

She cut me off. "My guidance counselor left a note in my locker requesting an urgent meeting."

"It makes no—"

Her voice rose as she talked right over my objection. "Someone chalked a message on my homeroom blackboard nominating me for the Friends of Rosie O'Donnell Society."

"Mills—"

"And the Science Club voted unanimously, except for Jimmy, to hold emergency elections to name new officers. They're kicking me out!"

The last word was more like an anguished cry.

"Bugger." I didn't know what else to say, because I realized in that instant, I'm not very good at consoling people.

"Do you know how bad that's gonna look? I could lose my scholarship . . . my freaking scholarship!"

"You don't need those people, Mills. They are insects—slime."

She lurched around me like a deranged chicken—arms flapping, eyes bulging. I genuinely felt for her. What could I do? "Do you want to go outside and walk or something?" (Could I be any more feeble?)

"Look, Amanda, I know it's not your fault, and you're being smeared too, but this kind of garbage evidently rolls right off your feathers."

My feathers?

"Maybe you're tougher than I am; maybe you don't care about anything." She stopped pacing. Her eyes bore in. "The fact is, everything I've worked for is on the line. I know you've got problems—bigger than mine, no doubt." (She didn't know the half of it, but now was certainly not the time to tell her.) "And . . . and I'm sorry about that. It's just . . . I don't think we should be seen together anymore. I—please, just stay away from me in school." She turned and walked out the front door.

I was about to defend myself when I remembered all the occasions I'd gotten away with malicious mischief. I doubt I'd ever truly understood the concept of irony before that moment. Here I was, hiding in a strange house from a pack of murderers, with a man who may or may not have taken sides against me, while being falsely accused of sexual pantheism, plus my only friend turns her back on me, and this time—I hadn't done anything wrong.

CHAPTER 19

Me—Plotting

In the past, I would have taken a glass of wine to steady myself, but that life seemed a million miles away. Then, I remembered Connie kept brandy in the kitchen.

"No," I said.

This was not the time to muddle my brain. From now on I was going to be focused. . . . NO MORE ALCOHOL!

Think.

I could always go to the FBI and ask for their protection. Let's see, how would that go. . . . (If my life were a movie, this is where dramatic music would fade up.)

DISSOLVE TO:

INTERIOR FBI OFFICES: OMAHA—DAY

VICTORIA VAN WYCK, a fascinating, intelligent, young woman [it's *my* movie] sits opposite AGENT HOOVER inside a small interview room.

AGENT HOOVER: Let me get this straight, Ms. Van Wyck.

VVW: You may call me Victoria.

AGENT HOOVER (Blushing): You entered the U.S. illegally on a forged passport under an assumed name—correct?

VVW: I had to.

AGENT HOOVER: Passport alteration is a federal offense punishable by up to ten years in prison. Also, there's a history of illegal consumption. You're a minor, Ms. Van Wyck—that's another year. Not to mention underage gambling, alteration of school transcripts, and a general disrespect for authority.

Stop the music. Get the picture? The authorities weren't going to help until after my death. That's the way the police work. Comforting, isn't it? Wait. I could fly to Switzerland, go back to the casino, pick up my twenty-one thousand dollars, and hire a full-time bodyguard. . . .

How dumb is that?

The problem had shaken down to Adam. Who's side had he chosen? How could I find out without tipping my hand? Like it or not, when he came home, I would have to confront him.

At six-thirty, he pulled into the driveway. I was alone in the house.

I met him at the door to our bungalow with a smile smeared across my lying lips. "Hey there, Uncle Bob, how was work?"

He slowed, then stopped, confusion chasing uncertainty across his face. "Fine . . . speaking of which, aren't you supposed to be at the library?"

I followed him into his bedroom and watched while he stowed a new leather briefcase in the closet. Curious. On the metal clasp the initials A.Y. were engraved. He seemed uneasy, so I smiled again. (As a general rule, friendly facial expressions are a girl's most effective weapon. A fetching grin or a sparkle-toothed smile disarms your opponent, making it easier to slip the dagger in.)

"Temporary seasonal layoff. I should be back on the job in a week or two."

He hung his jacket on a wooden hanger, loosened his tie, then fixed me with his grown-up stare. "Gives you a chance to catch up on your homework, then." He turned as if to dismiss me, but I had yet to play my card.

"Maybe I could come work at your office, part-time."

"I'm afraid that wouldn't be possible."

"Why not? You've got a secretary, right? I could help her."

He whirled, gathering himself. "First of all, I'm not in a position to hire or fire; second, how would you get back and forth to Omaha; and third, since when are you so keen on working, Amanda?"

I pouted. (When in doubt, pout. Make the grown-up think they've wounded your ever-so-tender adolescent feelings. It rattles the smug adult ego, and is a perfect conversation ender—always desirable.)

"You don't have to be so mean. . . ."

"I wasn't being—"

"May I have the car keys, please."

"Yes, you may."

Fishing the key ring from a trouser pocket, he handed it over. His eyes narrowed, searching mine for some hint of my intent.

"Thank you," I said.

Pivoting on my heel, I walked from his room, out of our house, down the driveway, into the car, and drove straight to Dupli-key. I smiled the whole way.

CHAPTER 20

Me and My Ally

That night, I locked my bedroom door and jammed it with a chair. I secured the wooden window shutters, and slipped into bed to read. The words ran together in one long jumble: *Tractlawprovidesthebasisuponwhichsettlersweregrantedland.* . . .

I turned out the light, but my thoughts galloped. My body started to tingle. I kept seeing the face of the scar-eyed assassin as Mills's words played over the image like an out-of-sync movie: "Maybe you don't care about anything . . . maybe you don't care about anything . . . care about anything . . . about . . . anything."

Over and over.

I put the pillow around my ears and sang to myself in order to drown out the roar. "Words can't bring you down . . . because you're beautiful."

Hour after hour.

Sometime after three AM I drifted off to sleep . . . crying, I think.

The next morning I was out of the house before anyone. I didn't feel up to facing Mills.

I walked a half mile and waited to catch the school bus. When it came, I sat in the last row and pulled my coat around my face.

In homeroom, I got a nasty surprise. Mr. Wilbury (remember him?) marched into the room thirty seconds after the opening bell sounded.

"Ms. Jones? Will you come with me, please?"

As I stood, the "Woo" chorus started from Vance and his crowd.

On the way out, I showed them one of my fingers (you can guess which one). I followed Wilbury down the hall to the principal's office. We stepped inside without a sound passing between us.

"Ms. Jones," Hart began, "word has come down to me about an assault in the school cafeteria the other day. Your name was mentioned. Any comments?"

The two gaped at me like hangmen. This, of course, really set me off. So, it was going to be an execution. Fine. Not mine though.

"I was taught that a gentleman offered a seat to a

lady when she entered the room." (That blew their hair back. Not Wilbury's; he was practically bald.)

"Um, er, take a seat, Ms. Jones," the principal mumbled.

"Thank you. As to the incident in the cafeteria, the only assault occurred when Noreen and her partner attacked me with a camera, and accused Millicent Hennigan and me—falsely—of sexual misconduct."

Hart shifted uneasily in his chair. Wilbury, standing beside me, looked away.

"I offered Noreen's partner, Darla, a handful of mashed potatoes to calm her; then Millicent and I left."

"Ms. Jones, that's not the way—"

I leapt to my feet. "As I'm sure you recall, I brought these scurrilous rumors to your attention a week ago, and you chose to do nothing."

"Just a minute—," he tried.

I cut him off. "When a school allows one group of students to victimize another, only bad things can result. Scandal, bad publicity, faculty firings . . ." I let the words sink in.

Wilbury blanched; the principal squeezed his monogrammed pen.

"I, on the other hand, am not afraid of bad publicity." I smiled. "You cannot possibly imagine how much of it I have endured. But Millicent and I are the victims here, and no one has lifted a finger to help us—including this school's administration."

They both coughed as if on cue. This was the moment . . . were they going to cave?

"I am not a vindictive person by nature," I purred. "I'm willing to let this whole sordid business go by the boards—" Wilbury's face lit up like a prisoner who's been offered a pardon.

"On the condition," I continued, "that this harassment stop, and that Millicent be restored in good graces to her club and committee appointments." I exhaled contemptuously. Their eyes followed every move. "After all, Wahoo High School is all about fairness, right?"

"Absolutely." The principal rose from his chair and offered me his hand. I refused, of course.

At the door, I turned back to them for a parting shot. "Go Bulldogs."

I walked out of the administrative offices and down the empty hallway, still not quite believing I'd pulled it off. But instead of feeling elation, the queerest thing happened. My legs became jelly; my stomach heaved. I felt flushed as I fell to my knees. What was wrong?

I could not bear to let anyone see me in this state, so after just a few deep breaths, I pulled myself up and staggered into the women's bathroom. I'd barely made it to the first stall before I heaved my insides out.

"Bleehh . . . blaach!"

It was disgusting. Classic stress reaction. Then, I noticed a pair of blue-stockinged legs in the adjacent stall. Soon, an upside down face appeared beneath the barrier.

It was a sophomore. "You awright?" she asked.

"Touch of bulimia," I answered. "And if you tell anyone about this, I'll cripple you."

Her head disappeared, the toilet flushed, and I heard footsteps scampering away.

I must have slumped there, retching, for a good ten minutes. Finally, the spasms passed. I felt weak but made it to the sink, where I splashed water onto my face, then reapplied gloss. (Rule #9: Never go anywhere without lip gloss and a comb tucked away in a pocket. Always *look* fresh, even if you feel like stale toast.)

I opened the frosted-glass window and breathed in cold air. After a few seconds, the oxygen and the sounds of activity from the athletic fields revived me completely.

I glanced at my watch—eighteen minutes 'til the end of first period. There was still time if I acted quickly. . . .

I knocked on the door to the teachers' lounge, and peeked inside. I was in luck. Several teachers "lounged" on fatigued leather chairs, or huddled around a tired coffeemaker. Mr. Moore sat by himself in the near corner, reading Proust.

"Psst," I actually said.

He looked up at me, then stood with a crooked grin when I motioned. "What are you doing out of class? Making mischief, I suppose." He stepped into the hall.

"I won't be making anything if you don't help me."

Two minutes later, we were inside his empty classroom. He locked the door and sat on the desk while I paced. "Go ahead," he said.

I told him everything: who I was, how I'd gotten to Wahoo and why—I even trotted out my favorite newspaper clipping of me, which I keep in my purse at all times, showing me surrounded by paparazzi, waving to an adoring crowd on the steps of a London courthouse. I looked smashing. And of course, I told him about Adam and the terrorist with the scar.

He stared out the window for the longest time. "Are you absolutely sure it was the same man—scar face?"

RINNNG!

The sudden sound of the school bell startled me. I must have jumped a foot.

"Do you know the coffee shop on Main, south of town?" he asked.

I nodded.

"Meet me there after school." He put his hand on my shoulder to comfort me. "Don't worry, we'll muddle through this." Then he was gone.

I felt as though my feet were cemented to the floor. Why couldn't I move? A group of students bustled inside, laughing and whooping.

The last thing I wanted to face was French or Biology with Darla and mashed-potato Noreen. But cutting classes after the scene I'd made with the principal and bald-eagle Wilbury would not have helped my cause. Plus, a note home to "Uncle Bob" might have stirred suspicion, or at the very least, activity. Let sleeping dogs snore. . . .

A group of junior boys jostled past me. "You're not welcome here," one of them said.

I stuck out my jaw, held my head high, and strolled out. (Never underestimate the power of anger to help you get through unpleasant situations. When someone challenges you, shut them up with positive action.)

French with Madame went as I expected—without her even acknowledging my presence. I used the time to plan a strategy, something at which I was becoming accomplished. (Perhaps I was a famous general in another life . . . Joan of Arc—wait, didn't they burn her at the stake? Never mind.)

In Biology, neither Noreen nor Darla made an appearance. Hooray for small favors. On the negative side, the teacher called on me twice with questions I could not answer—bad kitty.

"Ms. Jones, electrical stimuli producing movement in dead creatures is what?"

"Umm . . ."

"Galvanic skin response," she answered. "It was in your assignment. Didn't you read it?"

Titters from the rest of the class. "Some of us may need to buckle down and study a little more."

(Yes. And some of us may need depilatory on their upper lip!)

The bell ending class was about to sound when the P.A. snapped to life. It was Old Stone Face himself—Mr. Hart.

"Attention all students . . . the Wahoo Code of Behavior Handbook, which I'm certain all of you have read . . ."

A schoolwide groan and many mutterings arose.

"Section 11, paragraph 4, specifically bars sexual discrimination of any kind. This includes the spreading or dissemination of rumors designed to bring ridicule.

The punishment for violating this code is suspension or possible expulsion. . . ."

The laughter in the classroom dried up like a snail on a salt lick. Some of my classmates cut cautious glances at me. Even the teacher looked in my direction.

The principal droned on. "I have spoken, or will speak, to every member of the faculty on this matter, and the school policy will be zero tolerance for infractions."

I leaned back in my chair, trying not to appear too smug, but I must say I was enjoying the moment. I wondered how Mills was taking it.

"In conclusion, I want us all to work together in furtherance of the proud tradition of Wahoo High School. And don't forget the game against Wasatch this Saturday, featuring our undefeated Bulldogs! See you there."

The teacher clapped and most of the students joined halfheartedly. I marveled at what a perfect, mealy-mouthed political speech it had been. Principal Hart condemned the discrimination, while praising the ones who'd committed it.

CHAPTER 21

Me, Alive

I skipped the lunchroom, sitting high in the stadium bleachers to eat my apple, while I watched the track team run, jump, and perspire. If I had to be any kind of athlete, I'd choose track, I guess, because of the graceful movement. But the sweating part—no, thank you. Why doesn't someone invent a sport where you don't have to sweat? Wait, they already have. Golf . . . boring.

I hid out in study hall for the rest of the afternoon. At the final bell I hurried outside, heading for my coffee shop rendezvous with Huell Moore. When I arrived, he was already there, sitting alone at a booth in the back.

This place was the closest thing to offbeat in Wahoo. It featured incense, drapes made of colored beads, and mocha-colored walls displaying portraits of Jack Kerouac and James Dean.

"Sit down, Ms. Amanda," Huell said.

"Thank you."

"Do you take coffee?" he asked.

"I prefer tea."

"One double-espresso and one chai tea."

The waitress taking our order wore a denim skirt two sizes too small, and a flower-print peasant blouse.

"I've been thinking about your problem," Huell began, "but before I say anything, tell me, what would you like me to do?" His eyes shimmered, but there was strength in them. I knew my decision to trust him had been a good one.

Over tea and coffee, I poured out my plan using Adam's duplicate keys, and my knowledge of his office location. Huell would create a diversion with the receptionist while I tripped the fire alarm. When Adam and everyone else evacuated, I would sneak back in, open his desk with the duplicate keys, download his computer, sneak back out, and meet Huell outside in a pre-arranged getaway spot. . . . Brilliant, yes?

Huell took a long sip from his cup, his eyebrows twitching like St. Vitus Dance.

"Too elaborate. Good strategy, like good fiction, should be simple and direct."

I couldn't help but feel a twinge of disappointment.

"Here is my idea," he continued. "If Adam is intent upon your destruction by secretly allying himself with one of your father's would-be assassins, then the way to checkmate this ambition seems breathtakingly obvious."

He smiled and peered at me, awaiting my reaction. I'm not dense, as you know, but I was completely clueless to his meaning. I suppose I stared at him blankly.

"Oh, come now. Think like a writer, Amanda. Secrecy is the key for him. If Adam knows that others know of his plan, he can't murder you, or even allow you to be murdered, lest he face the gallows himself."

(I could have kissed Mr. Moore, but since he was a teacher and gay, I'm almost positive he wouldn't have enjoyed it.) "But if I tell Adam I know his plan—"

"Not you, silly," he interrupted, "me. Let us compose a note. He wrote on his napkin.

Adam, you have been seen in Omaha with the scar-faced assassin. Photographs of the two of you together exist. If anything untoward should happen to any of the Van Wycks, copies of these photos along with this note will receive generous distribution among law enforcement agencies.

I laughed. Then I began to sob with relief. I was not going to be murdered after all. Huell patted my hand, and spoke gentle words.

"Calm yourself, Miss Thing. Don't worry, I'll deliver the note personally, accompanied by two or three of my gym friends. He won't know who we are, or how we know, but I'm certain it'll put a bee in his bonnet. See what I mean about simplicity?"

He rose and flipped a five dollar bill onto the table. "By the way, how's that composition you promised me coming along?" This time he smiled, but I was too overcome with gratitude to respond.

"See you in class." He strolled through the beaded curtain and out of the shop.

CHAPTER 22

Friends

I walked home in a daze—two and a half miles—not feeling the wind or noticing the cars speeding by, unaffected by the frigid autumn sunset . . . yet I heard my own heartbeat for the first time. Marvelous.

Believing you might die, then being pulled from the volcano at the last minute, changes a person. I still wasn't out of the frying pan (mixing metaphors is fun—try it sometime), but the way was becoming clearer.

When I arrived home, I went to my room, locked the door, opened my math book, and dug in. It must have been well after nine PM. when I heard tapping on the shuttered window. I opened a louver and peeped out. Mills beckoned me outside.

The living room was dark as I opened my bedroom door. Adam's quarters sat empty. Evidently, he hadn't come home yet. I turned on the hanging lamp in the corner, pulled on my coat, and walked out. Mills stood at the bottom of the steps. Behind her, at a distance, I could see her mother puttering around in the kitchen. The warmth was inviting.

"Let's go someplace we can talk," Mills said.

"What will we talk about?"

"About what a jerk I am." She smiled, a timid, little grin.

All my anger at her rejection of me the day before seemed to slip away—but I didn't let her see that. (Rule #8: Don't forgive too easily; it encourages bad behavior.)

"So it's going to be a *long* conversation," I teased.

She laughed, then pulled her left arm from behind her, revealing a gift-wrapped box. "Don't get too excited. It's Godiva chocolate."

I took the box and followed her to the side of the house where the woodshed stood. She opened the creaky door and turned on a Coleman lantern.

Stacks and stacks of neatly sawed maple logs lined the walls, while pinewood kindling lay upon the dirt floor in the middle of the room. Off to the side, beneath the flickering lantern, two rickety wooden rocking chairs stood face-to-face.

She sat in one and gestured for me to sit opposite.

"Mom and I come out here sometimes to talk and smell the pine . . . it's therapeutic."

I grunted, "Mmmm."

"Let me start by saying how sorry I am for what I said—the way I treated you yesterday."

I didn't look at her, focusing my attention instead on unwrapping the little golden box.

"I wouldn't blame you," she continued, "if you never forgave me or even spoke to me again. I was a real turd."

A neutral glance in her direction, then back to the box. (Another thing I do is let people talk themselves into a blather. It makes them easier to manage.)

"My only excuse—and I know this is weak—but I panicked . . . losing my place on committees, the whole guidance counselor thing . . . I . . . I was selfish, and . . . and I underestimated your incredible, amazing, unbelievable genius."

She leapt from the chair and threw her arms around me, squeezing so hard I wheezed. She released me and sat back down.

"Thank you. Thank you thank you thank you thank you! I promise I'll never doubt you again. If you say the moon is made of blue cheese, I'll buy two slices!"

She throbbed with excitement. "How did you do it?" she gushed. "I mean, I know you went to the principal's office, goofy old Wilbury told me that, but what did you say? Did you bribe them? Beat them? You know, of course, that after the big "no picking on Mills and Amanda" announcement, they called me in and told me all my committee chairmanships would be reinstated. You knew that, right? Here."

She snatched the box from my hand in her excitement, ripped open the paper, then thrust it back at me. "Well, how'd you manage it?"

I took a deep breath—dramatic pause. "I simply pointed out that it was in their best interest to do the right thing."

Mills's voice fell an octave and she lowered her gaze. "So you're . . . you're not still mad at me."

"If I say I'm not, do you promise not to squeeze me anymore?"

She giggled and squeezed herself instead. "Victoria Van Wyck, you are a piece of work. They broke the mold when they made you." She jumped up. "Let's make a run to the state line, get some wine, and celebrate. I'm buying."

Ordinarily, I would have already been out the door and on the way. Party! But after the events of the day, I wasn't too surprised to hear myself say, "It's a school night, Mills, and I'm a little tired. Besides, I quit drinking."

"You sure?" she asked.

The box contained two chocolate truffles. I plucked one out and bit into it. I offered her the other and her smile lit up like Christmas.

"Just help me with my algebra homework on the weekends. And lighten up a little. Deal?"

She nodded. We were pals again. "Deal."

She gobbled down the sweet, and I found myself saying the most extraordinary thing: "Thanks."

A word about friendship. Generally, I believe friends are overrated. You meet someone, bond over common interests or shared enemies and spend time together— until one or both of you find new friends, move away, move on, have an argument, or just get bored. If you're not careful, these friendship "breakups" can give you the blues. Avoid this by maintaining perspective. If you make only one true, enduring friend your whole life, consider yourself fortunate.

I had Stella, of course, except when she had a really cute rich guy around—in which case she would disappear like Casper the ghost.

I began to let myself hope I'd found another in the person of Millicent Hennigan.

The next day, school felt altogether different. There were still furtive glances in my direction, but few rude comments. Mills and I sat together at lunch, and no one paid any attention. Jimmy and his crowd of eggheads joined us and told dumb, dirty jokes.

I laughed, don't ask me why.

CHAPTER 23

Huell Comes Through

It's a funny thing, time is. Einstein might have explained his relativity theory by saying: "Five minutes in a boring classroom seems like an hour, but an hour doing something you like seems like no time at all."

That's what the school year at Wahoo had become. Even my life as a Midwestern girl-next-door was no longer unbearable. I'm not saying my world had suddenly transformed into a Häagen-Dazs sundae with a cherry on top, but the days merged, one to the other, in a haze of school, homework, the library (I got my job back from Mrs. Brath, but made her keep the letter, just in case), sleep, movies on the weekend, and hanging with Mills.

And don't forget Huell Moore, who says I might

have "the right stuff," whatever that is, to become a writer someday. His door is always open to me. He tells wickedly funny stories about trust and betrayal, and is the only grown-up I've ever met I can talk to without using adult-speak. Here's an example of a Huell story he calls "The Parable of the Pilgrim."

A humble pilgrim goes on a long journey to find true love. Only a few miles from his destination, the pilgrim comes to a wide, swift-flowing river, where he encounters a Philistine with a motorboat.

"Excuse me sir," the pilgrim says, "but I must get across that river in order to find true love, and I'm afraid I can't swim. Could you help me, please?"

"I'm a Philistine," the boat keeper replies. "I don't believe in true love."

"I'll pay you."

"But I've only got enough gas for one complete trip across," the Philistine demurs.

"I'll give you everything I've got, and you can accompany me on my journey once we reach the other side."

"I told you, I don't believe in true love."

"But you'll have all my goods, my undying gratitude, plus a chance to explore the world beyond this river." The pilgrim is determined, you see.

"All right, hand over your money, and hop in."

The pilgrim jumps into the boat, and away they sputter. But halfway across, the Philistine cuts the engine and pushes the pilgrim into the dark water.

"Help me, boatman, for I will surely drown."

In answer, the boat turns back toward its original mooring. As the pilgrim starts to go under for the last time, he shouts, "But why? Why?"

"Shut up, pilgrim. You knew I was a Philistine when you made the bargain."

The other students in creative writing laughed when Huell finished, but I found it . . . sad. (Because I identified with Pilgrim? With the Philistine? Because I heard echoes of my own life within the parable? Because I'm getting soft and mushy in the head?)

Oh, by the way, a week after my coffee shop talk with Huell, Adam knocked on my door early one school morning.

"I don't know what you imagine my intentions toward you may be, but since I promised your parents I'd look after you, I have never wavered in that commitment, Victoria."

He was dressed in his blue suit, looking as serious as I'd ever seen him. T. S. Eliot popped into my head.

"Between the idea and reality falls the shadow," I said.

The expression on his face cracked, like a broken lightbulb. He composed himself, turned, and walked away without another word.

I tried to form a picture in my mind about what Huell's meeting with Adam must have looked like. . . .

Adam, working at his desk, hears the intercom buzz.

"Sir, there's a man here to see you . . . he says it's a matter of life or death."

"Send him in," Adam replies, not having a clue what awaits.

Huell enters . . . perhaps he's brought along three or four of his gym friends. (I picture five large men with amazing muscles and perfectly coiffed hair. They'd all be wearing tight t-shirts, of course, and flat-front dress slacks.)

Huell would hand over the letter, and Adam would read it without emotion.

"Have a nice day," Huell would say as he led his "posse" away.

Oh, I wish I'd been a fly on that wall!

Toward the middle of November, the junior and senior classes combined to host a rally in the auditorium, at which each Harvest Queen candidate was to give a two-minute speech stating why she should be elected.

Jimmy and his crowd, along with Mills and the other brains, had been getting out the vote for me all around school, touting me as the "un-candidate."

Our slogan: "Sick of the in-crowd? Vote Amanda."

In spite of their best efforts, I detected no groundswell of support. Since the principal's P.A. speech, in fact, few students talked to me. Many times, people even went out of their way to avoid eye contact. Naturally, I stared at them until they looked back. Being an outcast was more fun than I'd imagined it could be.

The day of the rally I was so nervous at the thought of speaking to the entire assembly, I couldn't sit still or concentrate for even a second. (Try to imagine how you'd feel, addressing 450 people who hate your guts.)

Finally, just before fourth period, the moment came, and every student in Wahoo High filed into the auditorium. The atmosphere was electric. Placards and flags waved like white caps on a stormy sea—some even bore my name. Misty, Dawn, and I sat in chairs on the stage as the mob flowed in.

Mr. Hart sat beside us, then rose to the microphone and called for quiet. I could feel my breath coming in shallow bursts, my knees knocking like maracas. A hush fell upon the rabble.

"The first candidate for this year's Harvest Queen is new to Wahoo High." A buzz of anticipation swept all the way from back to front. "Please give a warm welcome and your kind attention to Ms. Amanda Jones."

Silence.

That's when I knew I'd be all right. They were trying to freeze me. Fine. Let them. Icy detachment flooded my brain. My legs suddenly felt strong. (You've heard the stories of old ladies who lift school buses to save the children inside, or little girls who pull their mothers from frozen lakes? At that moment, I could have bitten a nail in half.)

When I stood, I heard Mills, Jimmy, and a few others (very few) clapping. The sound they made was thin in the cavernous room, but to me, their encouragement was as big as a brass band.

I stepped to the microphone, looked down at Vance, Skeeter, and the football gang jamming the first two rows, and I smiled. "Most of you hate me. . . . I wonder if you even know why."

Silence. Time seemed to freeze. No one moved or even breathed.

"Because some big shot turned me into a stereotype?"

"You suck!"

Somebody from the front row yelled this, causing a cascade of boos. Were they booing me or the heckler? The principal stood, his face as red as a carnival balloon. He advanced toward the microphone, but I warned him off.

"Don't bother, I'm almost done." The booing stopped as suddenly as it began. I could even hear a few laughs.

My gaze settled on Mills, sitting in the back of the audience, clutching a GO AMANDA banner. I winked at her, and she nodded encouragement.

"You may not believe it, but before I came here, winning a contest like this would have meant a lot to me. Now I see that it doesn't matter at all, which is why I'm withdrawing my candidacy."

The room was so still you could have heard a butterfly sneeze.

I flashed my twenty-four-carat smile at the front row. "Oh, and one more thing . . . have a great day."

I turned and strode past Mr. Hart without so much as a backward glance.

The boos came again, but not as many, and there was actually some clapping.

Backstage, I heard Misty's voice at the mic. "Thank God that's over."

Huge applause . . . CHEERS.

Doesn't matter, I thought. I said what I had to say. (And how often can you say that?) I pushed open the emergency exit, and stepped outside. It began to snow.

CHAPTER 24

Mills, Not Me

The ballots for Harvest Queen were counted on Thursday so "Her Majesty" could get ready for the parade. Misty received 264 votes, Dawn 151, and I got 37.

Even though I lost, something new had been jumpstarted by my appearance onstage . . . an undercurrent of what? Acceptance? People that I didn't know passed me in the hallway and chirped cheerful greetings.

"Hello, Amanda."

"Hey, Mandy."

"Hi."

"How are ya?"

My favorite came from a redheaded sophomore who greeted me every day, outside Algebra.

"What's the haps, Mandoid?" Every single day. Like we'd been friends all our lives.

Mandoid?

(I later discovered his name was Redmond Michael Butts! Parents can be so stupid. Think about going through life with the name Red Butts. Puh-leeze.)

The school year raced by, and soon, midterms were on everyone's mind. (Yes, mine too.) I had decided to try to do well on them—not that I didn't usually—*au contraire.* Even doing as little homework as possible and taking into account my, shall we say, cavalier attendance record, I had always finished in the top third of my class at L'École Suisse. The point is, I really wanted to score big. Why? Who knows. Maybe Mills' and Jimmy's competition had rubbed off on me. Perhaps I was "sublimating," as my analyst would say. Could be I was just bored—whatever. This time I was determined.

The exam everyone said would be toughest was Advanced American History; the one class Mills and I shared . . . and it was shaping up as a real showdown. Last woman standing wins. It's a competitive world— get used to it. If I were ever hired to compose a slogan for today's teen girl, I'd say: "Just win, baby!"

So, until December 21—exam day—I was using every spare minute to prepare: homeroom, lunch, the library. Mrs. Brath caught me studying on the job and occasionally chided me about it.

"I guess the state of Nebraska is already subsidizing you, since you're getting paid to do nothing!"

She tried to hide it, but I knew she liked me. It's my sparkling personality, of course.

Sometimes I even studied for other classes while sitting in French. Madame was probably relieved I was no longer raising my hand to answer questions. *Zut alors!*

By the way, I sent off for college brochures, and no, you may not know which ones: a) because it's bad luck to talk about it, and b) I can't afford to go to any of them.

Every time I think about money it depresses me. I'm not whining, but poverty sucks.

Melancholy memory . . . when I was fourteen, my parents took me with them for the only vacation we ever spent together. The island of St. Martin in the Caribbean. The Dutch side—called St. Maarten—has better hotels and casinos, but the French side has better restaurants and jewelry stores. I think Father's company was acquiring one of the restaurants, so we stayed "avec les Français."

Mostly, Father did business, which left Mumsie and me on our own. The third day, we went shopping. My parents had argued that morning. Again. I think the subject was him working so much. Mother was in a black mood.

The moment we walked into Cartier, she demanded to see the manager.

"Oui, madame," he said, bowing and stroking his pencil mustache.

"I should like to see the most expensive bracelet you carry."

The little man's eyes glittered like black pearls.

"I feel extravagant today," she added.

"But of course, madame."

Within three minutes, she'd purchased an emerald-and-diamond wristlet for ninety-thousand dollars, and a jewel-encrusted watch for me (cost: thirty-five thousand).

"That should get his attention," Mother whispered as we walked outside.

"Whose?" I thought, the manager's or Father's?

Why am I telling you this boring story filled with psychological symbolism?

Let me finish.

We went to lunch, and as we were ready to leave, I retired to the restroom to refresh. I took off the new watch, put it on the counter so as not to get it wet, and promptly forgot it.

It wasn't until several blocks later, Mother discovered the loss. "Where's your watch?"

"Omigod," I screamed, pelting back to the restaurant.

My pretty bauble was gone, of course.

When I re-emerged and told Mother, she gasped, then slapped me across the face—the only time she has ever struck me.

"That's what I feel when you treat my gifts so carelessly."

I have never forgotten that slap in front of the little restaurant named Ma Maison—my house.

What does it mean? I don't know. A psychiatrist would say, "What do you think it means?"

Just a snapshot of the lives of the rich and restless.

The weekend before exams, someone came knocking at my window at one AM. I had fallen asleep with the light on, fully clothed, reading—what else—American history, so when the tapping came, I woke up disoriented.

"Wha—what?"

"Shh, it's me," she whispered.

When I peeked out the window, I saw Mills standing in a foot of fresh snow.

"Put your jacket and boots on. We have to talk."

Something in her manner said trouble, so I donned

outerwear and climbed outside. "Are you cracking up? It's freezing out here."

She pulled me through the snow to the woodshed. There was no moon. The black sky twinkled with a million cold stars. It was so clean and beautiful, I resolved then and there to study astronomy one day. Inside the shed, we stamped the snow off our boots and turned on the lantern. The smell of fresh pine needles filled my head.

An opossum lurched past, scaring me half to death. Now I was annoyed. "What's going on? You know it's a school day tomorrow?"

"I'm sorry, but I was with Jimmy and . . . and I think I messed up—big-time—and . . . and . . ."

I could see in this flickering light, she was almost crying.

"And . . . you're my best friend—you've got to help me, Amanda!"

Suddenly, I wasn't cold or annoyed. A warmth seeped through my chest, reddening my face. (Did she just call me her "best friend"?)

"Of course I'll help you. Got any money?" My little joke landed with a *thud*.

Mills wrung her hands and fidgeted. It must be serious, I thought.

"I don't know where to start—okay, I'll just say it. Jimmy and I . . . me and Jimmy . . ."

I knew what she was going to say.

"We were parked in his car, you know . . . after studying, and we started . . . um . . . kissing. It got a little heavy. . . ."

She was so agitated, she couldn't stand still. I didn't know what to think. "Did he try to force you?"

"No, no, no, I wanted to!"

"I don't understand. What happened?"

"I pushed him away and said, 'I can't afford to be distracted.' "

She burst into tears and started hitting herself on the head with her mittens. If I live to be five hundred, I'll never be more surprised than I was at that moment.

"Um . . . er . . . take it easy," I said. (Sometimes I'm such a lame-o!)

"Oh, Victoria, the look on his face . . . I crushed him. Can you believe how selfish I am—our first make-out, and I ruined it. He'll never speak to me again. I'm an idiot!"

She whapped herself, cried, talked, then started the cycle over. "I'm the stupidest girl who ever lived. I don't deserve a boyfriend." *Whap! Whap! Whap!* "What am I gonna do?" *Whap!* "And don't say it doesn't matter, 'cause it does!"

"I can't think while you're hitting yourself. Stop, okay?"

She finally sat, hiding her face in her coat.

"You may not know this," I began, "but I've actually never gone all the way."

She looked up. "You lie. Really?"

"The point being, boys keep coming back anyway."

"He drove me home," she said, wiping her eyes with battered mittens. "When we arrived, he put his arms around me and said, 'You're the perfect woman.' He was trying to tell me he loved me, and I got out and slammed the door. Stupid!"

"No one's ever loved me before." (The words just slipped out of my mouth. I actually had to clamp down to keep from crying too. I think something's wrong with me.)

"Amanda, you've got to talk to him. You're so . . . sophisticated. Make him understand. Promise me?"

"I promise," I said, but I never felt less sophisticated in my life.

CHAPTER 25

It's Not Always
about Me

Next morning, everyone in both households awoke early. Adam prepared a big breakfast: Canadian bacon, mushroom omelets, fresh fruit, coffee, tea, and biscuits. (I admit I waited until he took a bite before I did—just in case.)

"So what's new with our two all-star scholars?" Connie asked.

Mills and I exchanged a look, then answered in unison, "Nothing."

Adam had already put snow chains on the Hennigan truck so Connie could drive us to school. It was bizarre, traveling through miles of flat farmland covered in a thick white blanket. None of us spoke until we arrived at the school's frigid front entrance.

"Bye, Ms. Hennigan."

"Bye, Mom."

She drove off, and Mills grabbed my arm. "Remember, the moment you see Jimmy, jump him if you have to, but make him listen."

"Right. I'll tie him up. I'm *sophisticated*."

"Gotta go. I'm counting on you." She scurried inside.

I stood next to a snowdrift, watching early-morning students shuffle past. They all wore the same blank expression. Science tells us that each snowflake is unique, just as every human being is. Honestly, I don't see that much difference in either.

After homeroom, I headed for my locker to pull out my biology text, when guess who spotted me?

"Mandy, hold up, will ya?" It was Jimmy, making a beeline through a crush of students.

Quick, think of something to say. What's his mood? He doesn't look angry. . . .

"Jimmy, how are you?" I smiled as if nothing were wrong.

"Have you seen Mills? We were supposed to hook up—I mean meet—not hook up . . . rendezvous, as you might say. But she never showed." His forehead scrunched, his lips contorted as if he were in great pain.

"Um . . . Jimmy, we have to talk." I tried to keep my voice soothing.

"She's not mad at me or anything, right?" He held his books to his chest, and I could see his hands were trembling. He was so pitiable I almost wanted to rub his ears, like a stray dog.

"Jimmy—," I started, then stopped, unsure how to continue. This was a delicate matter; there was probably only thirty seconds left before second period began, and every student in school seemed determined to jostle us in that hallway on their way to class.

"I blew it with her last night, didn't I?" He turned away, his head sinking to his chest. At any second, he might have burst into tears.

"Jimmy, I think Mills is in love with you."

His head jerked up, his eyes latched onto mine, his body becoming suddenly alert. I have never seen a human being look more energized.

A joyous *whoop* escaped his throat as he whirled and ran away down the hall, dodging teachers and students alike.

"She loves me!"

At lunch, Mills and Jimmy held hands in public for the first time, staring at each other, giggling, and feeding each other little bites of food.

By mid-December, they were talking about going to college together. Love is kind of silly, isn't it?

. . .

The night before midterms, the three of us studied our tails off in Mills's room. They'd taken to bringing me along on these sessions as a kind of chaperone—so you-know-what didn't happen again. I liked studying with them because Mills's algebra lessons sparkled, and Jimmy was a biology whiz. It was a good arrangement all around, since I was dragging them through French.

At 1:45 AM, Jimmy kissed Mills goodnight and drove home. I retired to my house. Adam was still awake, reading Tolstoy in the living room.

"Good luck tomorrow. Your parents would be proud of you."

These were the first words between us in a week. I closed and locked my door, got into bed, but I couldn't shut my mind off. Mum and Dad . . . it had been almost five months now. I'd gone long stretches before, not seeing them, but not like this. Were they all right? Did they miss me? Mother certainly, but Daddy? I couldn't remember the last time he said he loved me. For that matter, when was the last time I told them? Was I a bad daughter? What good is an algebraic field anyway?

When the alarm went off at 6:00, it seemed as though I hadn't slept at all. Across the breakfast table, Mills looked like I felt.

"Did you sleep?" she croaked.

"More like a fitful doze," I said.

"You're both gonna do fine." Connie's cheerful demeanor seemed discordant, given the pressure we were under.

We just glared at her.

The ride to school was a blur; homeroom became a rush of last-minute fact checking. Then it arrived. First exam . . . French. It was so easy, I could have laughed.

Analyze a long passage from Balzac, in French of course, and compose a French poem that both scans and rhymes. I decided to translate an old Buddhist proverb:

> *Many paths there be*
> *to scale the mountain's height*
> *But all who journey see*
> *the same moon's light.*

I finished well ahead of anyone else, put the paper on Madame's desk, and walked out, whistling.

Biology was a different kettle of fish guts altogether. Some of the formulations threw me, and my osmotic explanation wasn't as clear as I would have liked. . . . Oh, and Noreen and her döppleganger deskmate were cheating! They had crib notes written on their thighs. They pulled up their skirts whenever they needed an answer. So gross!

I didn't say anything. I was too busy with my own problems. I finished just before the bell and I thought: If I salvage a B, I'm way ahead. Next came—da, da, da, doom; da, da, da, doom—Algebra!

To my great surprise, I missed only one problem, as far as I knew. I'll bet Mills and Jimmy killed on their tests. Their help, especially Mills's, had pulled me through.

At lunch, the three of us compared notes. "I feel good. All in all, better than last year." Mills was positively beaming. Jimmy looked like a crash-test dummy. (He usually looks like that.)

"If you did better than last year, I give up. I'll never be number one."

Mills put her arms around him. "You're my number one, Jimmy-jam." Then she kissed him. Wet and sloppy.

"Hey," I said. "People are trying to eat here."

"They'd be better off Frenching than scarfing this food," Jimmy replied. "What kind of meat is that—roadkill?"

Mills and I walked out together after yet another Jimmy/ Millicent lip-lock. (Ugh.)

Next stop—American History. The AP midterm. Ace this, and my reputation would soar.

Mills and I were both so charged up, I don't think we spoke two words on the way. Inside class, the tension was unbearable. After all, this was the honors program.

"All right, students, open your test booklets. . . . Good luck."

I ripped and started in immediately. The first time I glanced at the clock, thirty minutes had elapsed, but I was more than half finished.

"Ms. Hennigan, would you pick up your test book and come with me, please."

I turned to see Mr. Wilbury tugging at Mills's jacket. What the—?

Mills whispered a reply—something about not being finished. For some reason, Wilbury was implacable. Mills slid from her seat and followed him out, but not without a panicky look in my direction. Whatever was going on was not good. Was it a death in the family? Not Connie, I hope! What should I do?

"Finish the test," I heard myself say the words out loud. Several students glanced over and grunted. I raced through the rest of the exam, put the booklet in the completed basket, and dashed out.

Running toward the principal's office, down the empty corridor, my imagination was on fire with implausible explanations. I reached the door just as the bell rang. I pushed inside and rushed up to the receptionist—sourpuss Mrs. What's-her-name.

"What's wrong with Millicent Hennigan? I have to know! Did somebody die?"

The old crone stared at me with dead eyes, shaking her head. What the hell did that mean? I was about to scream at her when the principal's inner office door swung open, and Mills trudged out. She was in tears.

"Mills, what happened?"

"They . . . they found a copy of the history exam in my . . . my . . . my . . ." She was too upset to get the words out.

"Notebook? Purse? Locker?" I tried.

"Locker," she echoed. "They say I've ch . . . ch . . . cheated!"

"Impossible."

"I'm expelled," she sobbed. "Mom's coming to get me." Her anguish was so palpable, it crept into my soul like psychic smallpox.

Everything she'd worked for—ruined. No scholarship. No college. Her life had literally crashed and burned in one terrible moment.

"Amanda, it's a lie! But . . . but . . . they won't believe me." She put her head on my shoulder, too ashamed to show her face.

"I'll make them believe you." As soon as I said it, I knew what I had to do. I pulled away, then barged into Hart's office. Wilbury and the principal had their plotting heads together when I burst in.

"You can't expel Millicent!"

"Get out of this office, young lady."

"You can't expel her," I shouted.

"She cheated. She knew the penalty for stealing an exam."

"She didn't, I tell you."

"And how do you know that?" The principal grinned at me with crocodile teeth.

"Because I stole the exam and put it in her locker to frame her."

CHAPTER 26

Life Will Surprise You

You can't ever really plan things in this life. No matter how clever or determined you are, or how meticulous the intention, something will always come along to knock your little choo-choo right off the track.

How did it happen? From sailing through midterm exams, and practically guaranteeing a 3.5 grade point average, I was sitting between Mills and her mom on the road home, expelled from school in disgrace. Wilbury and Hart had won—I was ruined. I'd saved my friend, but paid a terrible price.

Mills kept asking if I was okay, while Connie fussed, dividing her attention between the icy highway and me. I suppose I was in shock of some sort, not really hearing them, my own thoughts a blur. For the first time in my life, I realized that momentous decisions come upon all of us when least expected—and how you choose to act in a split second can affect your destiny forever.

I remember feeling numb. I think I said, "Just need to lie down a bit."

Then Mills put her arm around me, and I closed my eyes. As I drifted off, I heard her sniffle and say, "Bless you."

I woke up in my own bed, at sunset. My head throbbed, and it took me a few seconds to realize Mills, her mother, and Adam were looking down at me.

"I brought you some hot chocolate, sweetie. Try to drink," Connie said.

Mills handed me the mug and sat on the bed beside me. I drank.

"Thank you," I said.

"I just want you to know, I think what you did was the . . . the most courageous and selfless act I've ever known." Tears welled in Connie's eyes, and she clutched Adam's hand. I looked up at him and saw his usual steely determination staring back.

"I didn't cheat."

Mills squeezed my hand now. "She couldn't have; I'd stake my life on it."

"Hell's bells, I know that." Adam pulled up a chair and sat. "Whatever you may have been in the past, whatever faults you possess, cheating is not one of them. I'm damn proud of you, in fact."

"You . . . you are?" That was the last word I would ever have conceived Adam York saying to me. "Proud." Imagine.

Then he stood, his face hardened—business as usual. "Don't be so shocked. I'm on your side. Now get changed. I'm taking everyone out to dinner and a surprise."

He and Connie walked out. I realized I was still wearing my school clothes. Mills helped me up. I felt lightheaded, almost tipsy. Why had I ever enjoyed that feeling?

"What's got into him?" I asked.

Mills smiled. "He believes in you. Get dressed."

An hour later, we piled into the Taurus and drove to Omaha. Usually, I'm a bah-humbug sort of person, but as I noticed the Christmas lights shimmering all over the city, I found myself thinking: what a magical holiday. For a day or two, people actually try to be nice to one another. Mills was in a giddy mood, trying to cheer me up, so the two of us sat in the back singing yuletide carols with bawdy lyrics.

Silent fart
Holy fart
Smells so bad
Makes me sad

We started to giggle (why was I feeling so good?), then Connie and Adam joined in, to the tune of "Good King Wenceslas."

Big pimp Applesauce looked out
driving in his Lincoln
All his hos lay round about
Big and phat and stinkin'

We howled with laughter until our sides hurt. I found it odd somehow, to see Connie and Adam giggling in the front seat while slapping themselves like children on a field trip to the circus. Kinda sweet, actually.

Adam picked a restaurant called the Jockey Club—very chic. The maître d' wore a tailored dinner jacket, and actually spoke French with an impeccable accent. I requested the table next to the aquarium at the very back.

"Bien sûr, mademoiselle," he answered.

Dinner turned into a celebratory feast with crab

and seafood for starters. My mind was so pixilated, I wondered if the fish swimming inside the tank were watching and thinking: My God, these people are eating us!

I ordered osso buco, which was seared perfectly. Adam chose steak tartare (raw meat—figures). Connie got a heavenly bouillabaisse, and Mills—fettuccine Alfredo.

The food just kept coming—one course after another—salad, soup, cheese, fresh bread, and finally dessert. A whole trayful. This was costing a fortune! I noticed Adam checking his watch. Why, I wondered.

Finally, after none of us could eat another bite, Adam pulled six 100-dollar bills from his wallet and put them on the table. He glanced at his watch again, rose, and said, "Shall we go?"

For some reason the hair on the back of my neck stood up. Something was afoot, I could feel it.

Mills and Connie seemed relaxed, but I was wary as an alley cat following them out the door into the cold night parking lot. I stiffened at the sight of a long black limo idling at the curb. Adam walked right up to the passenger door.

"Mills—" I reached for her arm.

"What?" she said.

Then, as if in a slow motion sequence, the limo

doors swung open, and out stepped my mother and father.

"Mom! Daddy!" I cried.

The sound died in my throat. Stepping out from behind my parents were the two assassins—Mr. Scar-eye and his cohort, dressed in business suits. What did this mean? A setup? Impending death? A quick glance at Adam revealed him smiling contentedly.

"Victoria, come here, darling," Mother said.

Father, seeing the look of shock that must have contorted my expression, turned to the "assassins."

"Perhaps you two had better wait in the car."

"Oui, monsieur," Scar-eye said, and both disappeared into the limo.

What??? My mind locked up, this tableau too surreal to grasp. Mother wrapped me in her arms and began kissing me.

"Oh, sweetheart, I've missed you so. You've put on weight, dear. It suits you. Put your arms round and give Mummy a squeeze."

"Your mother's right. You look good." (Father calling me "you" again.)

I pulled clear of her embrace. "But ... but the killers—" I cut Adam a quick look. No reaction—the bastard.

"What—"

"Victoria, you'll have to forgive us, but I'm afraid that was all just a story, dear."

"You were out of control. We'd tried everything. . . ."

My ears burned. A roaring sound in my head drowned out all but a few of my father's words: "desperate" . . . "at our wit's end" . . . "drastic change" . . . "psychiatric intervention."

Then it sank in.

They had duped me.

All of it, the phony assassins who really worked for my father, the company trouble, the bogus Mafia plot, Adam, poverty—all fake!

I could feel the blood drain from my face. I must have screamed, since my parents recoiled in horror. I ran past them into the parking lot toward the Taurus. I had a spare key now. If only I could make it in time. . . .

Darting between moving cars, I found ours, jumped inside, and locked it just as Adam appeared, knocking on the window.

"It was for your own good, Vickie."

The engine roared to life. "I never want to speak to you again."

I accelerated and skidded out of the icy lot, leaving Adam, my parents, Mills, and her mother to recede in my rearview mirror.

. . .

Within minutes, I was on Interstate 80 headed east. If I kept going I could be in Des Moines in six or seven hours—twelve hours after that, Chicago. They'd never find me there. Whom did I know in Chicago? No one. Wait. I had friends in New York. I could drive there in two days. They'd help me . . . do what?

Snow flurries swirled around my windshield. The headlights from westbound traffic were like passing starbursts on a concrete sea. I let my mind tune in to the steady rhythm of the wiper blades as they swept snowflakes across the frigid glass.

SKRUNK.

SQUEAM.

SKRUNK.

SQUEAM.

Back and forth they went. Tirelessly. I wondered what it would be like to be born with only one purpose in life. Suddenly, I longed for simplicity.

Friends in New York . . . did I say? Okay, I *knew* two boys in New York: one in Manhattan, another on Long Island, both party brats from wealthy families whose only interest had been to attempt to feel me up. I felt a shiver trill my spine. Some friends.

The truth is, the only people who'd ever really cared for me (not my money or my body) were in Wahoo, a town I was now leaving for good. Mills, Connie—had they known? Were they part of it? No. Impossible. I would have sensed it. They were true friends, surely. And Mrs. Brath and Huell Moore, they'd wanted to help. I suppose even Adam, in his way, was trying to do the right thing . . . but he should have trusted me—damn him!

I was an hour past the Iowa border, making good time on a straight stretch of slushy road as I pulled off to buy gas. When I returned to the Interstate, I found my-self heading west. It was not a conscious decision. It just happened. I was going home.

I switched on the radio.

"Amazing grace, how sweet the sound, that saved a wretch like me. I once was lost, but now am found, was blind but now I see."

Do you know this song? It's an old American hymn. So beautiful. I am not a particularly religious person, but when that tune echoed inside my chilly car, I understood.

Mother, Father, and Adam did what they thought they had to. Now, I was about to do the same.

I pulled back into the Hennigan driveway a little after midnight. Several cars, Daddy's limo, and a police cruiser lined the front yard. Lights were on in the house, and I could see people milling about. When I turned off the engine and stepped outside, I noticed it had stopped snowing. The sky loomed crisp and clear. A full moon shone brightly, and I imagined it smiling down on me.

"It's Victoria!"

Mills's voice squealed from the front porch. She ran toward me, followed by Mom, Dad, Adam, Connie, Huell Moore, Mrs. Brath, her husband, Jimmy, and a few of his buddies.

Mills grabbed me and squeezed as if I were the Ancient Mariner returned from the sea. "Don't ever do that again," she scolded.

Then the mob was on me all at once, hugging, kissing, laughing, crying, and . . . well, you get the picture.

And here's the funny part: I was crying too . . . tears of joy.

EPILOGUE

Within a week, my father's investigators, working with the school principal, had cleared me of the cheating charges. (See, I told you being rich was an advantage.)

No one ever found out for certain who stole the test and stuck it in Mills's locker, but Skeeter, Vance, and several other footballers transferred out of Wahoo High at the beginning of the next semester. (Adam's work, I'm told.)

Mills was allowed to retake the exam, and she aced it, of course.

Adam went back to Lucerne with a promotion— head of Corporate Investigation. They say he'll make CEO one day, and I know he'll be a good one. Connie plans to visit him this summer.

As for me . . . I decided to stay in Wahoo and finish school. (Mom cried. Dad said, "Whatever you want.") To tell you the truth, the place is kinda growing on me.

Victoria Julianne Van Wyck
(Amanda Jones)

Rule #1:   Always keep them guessing.

Rule #2:   When adults start winning an argument by force of logic, immediately change the subject.

Rule #3:   Never underestimate your intuition. Treat your psychic feelings like the gifts they are, and they'll serve you forever. Ignore them, and they'll wither and die.

Rule #4:   Remember, "pretty" is something you put on when you need to—otherwise, cool it.

Rule #5:   Never be obvious with boys.

Rule #6:   Don't let adults get too deeply involved in your problems. It's like feeding pigeons—they'll never go away if you do.

Rule #7:   Use the guilt approach whenever possible: Adults are always guilty about something—why not let it be about how horribly they've treated you?

Rule #8:   Don't forgive too easily; it encourages bad behavior.

Rule #9: Never go anywhere without lip gloss and a comb tucked away in a pocket.

Rule #10: Never fall in love . . . unless you absolutely have to.

Rule #11: Always follow the rules—Victoria's rules.